KT-132-126

'Wonderfully expresses the grit and cosmopolitan glamour of Shanghai today ... In *Five Star Billionaire,* Mr Aw has achieved something remarkable' JULIA LOVELL, *Wall Street Journal*

'*Five Star Billionaire* is hard to beat' PICO IYER, *Time*

'This brash, teeming, explosive city is the real protagonist of Aw's richly observed and beautifully written novel' *The Times*

By the same author

The Harmony Silk Factory
Map of the Invisible World
We, The Survivors

COLLINS MODERN *CLASSICS*

THE BAGTHORPE SAGA
ORDINARY JACK

HELEN CRESSWELL

HarperCollins *Children's Books*

First published in Great Britain by Faber and Faber Ltd. in 1977
First published by HarperCollins *Children's Books* in 2017
HarperCollins *Children's Books* is a division of HarperCollins*Publishers* Ltd,
1 London Bridge Street
London SE1 9GF

The HarperCollins *Children's Books* website address is
www.harpercollins.co.uk

1

ISBN 978-0-00-821167-7

Typeset by Palimpsest Book Production Limited, Falkirk, Stirlingshire
Printed and bound in England by Clays Ltd, St Ives plc

To Brian, with love

Chapter One

WHEN ROSIE, WHO was only eight anyway, beat him doing ten lengths of the pool, it was the last straw. He didn't show he cared. He made such a point of sauntering carelessly to the dressing room that he skidded and went flat and everybody laughed. He forced himself to laugh as well, and only found the grazes on his elbows when he was towelling himself.

I got born in the wrong family, he thought, as he trudged back home alone over the fields. The others were still in the water, getting their money's worth.

Ordinary Jack, that's me. It's what they should've christened me – Ordinary Jack Matthew Bagthorpe – with an e.

There were four Bagthorpe children, and the other three were always winning prizes and medals, and William, the eldest, had got to the point where he was winning cups, silver ones, for the sideboard, and little shields with his name engraved on them.

You're immortal if your name gets put on cups and shields, thought Jack moodily. *I'll never be immortal.*

William's cups and shields were for tennis, and were bad enough in themselves, but what really rankled was that tennis was only the second String to William's Bow. (Most of the family had second Strings to their Bows, and some had three or even four. Strings to Bows were thick on the ground in the Bagthorpe household.) William's real speciality was electronics. He had put up an aerial thirty feet high in the vegetable garden and was in touch with a whole lot of radio hams all over the world including one called Anonymous, from Grimsby, who wouldn't give his real name. William said he was a pirate, which sounded fascinating, but he wouldn't let anyone else speak to him.

"A veil of secrecy must be preserved," he was fond of saying.

Jack, who would have given anything to be on speaking terms with a pirate from Grimsby, often felt like punching William when he said this.

Uncle Parker was dozing in a deckchair under the apple trees when Jack reached home.

"Hello, young Jack," he said, without opening his eyes.

There's another of them, Jack thought. *Can even see with his eyes shut.*

None the less, he liked Uncle Parker, who was not all that brilliant, and whose main distinction was that the way he drove his car was the talk of the neighbourhood (though he had never yet been prosecuted for it).

"If you could do anything in the world this afternoon, what would you do?" enquired Uncle Parker, his eyes still closed. This was another thing about him that Jack liked. He never said what you expected him to say.

"Be immortal," said Jack promptly.

"Bit pointless," observed Uncle Parker. "You're bound to survive the afternoon anyway, I should say. You can't be immortal just for an afternoon, you know, old son."

"I know that," said Jack, nettled. "It means to live for ever. Anyway, you asked me, and I told you."

"You won't get immortal piggling at your father's pansies," said Uncle Parker. "That I can tell you. More likely to get cut off in your prime."

Jack snatched away his hand which had admittedly, though quite of its own accord, been picking off pansy heads.

"It just shows what a nervous wreck I am," he said. "I already bite my nails, and say 'touch wood' all the time, and now I'm piggling pansies. Goodness knows how I'll end up."

"I suppose what you're all steamed up about as usual is not being a genius?"

Jack nodded. The two of them had had this kind of conversation before. Uncle Parker, not being a Blood Relation of the Bagthorpes, merely lucky enough to be married to Jack's Aunt Celia (who was not only ravishingly beautiful but could also solve *The Times* crossword in ten minutes flat without a dictionary and do pottery and poetry) could sympathise with Jack's feelings. On the other hand, whereas Uncle Parker did not seem to mind being everlastingly eclipsed, Jack did.

"What's been going on at the pool, then?" enquired Uncle Parker. "One of 'em do a triple somersault from the top board and get invited to the next Olympics, did they?"

"Rosie beat me doing ten lengths."

"Pooh!" said Uncle Parker.

"It's all right you saying 'Pooh!' You're not her brother, and older, and you won't hear them all going on at tea-time when she tells them."

"I shall, then," returned Uncle Parker. "We're stopping. Grandma's birthday, remember. And I shall say 'Pooh!' then, just as I say 'Pooh!' now."

"Will you? Will you really?"

"Naturally. You must have the courage of your convictions, Jack, old lad. If you mean 'Pooh!' then you must say 'Pooh!' and the devil take the consequences."

"But why do you mean 'Pooh'?" persisted Jack. "After all, it's pretty good – she is younger than me."

"If you'll forgive me saying so," said Uncle Parker, "the way you swim, just about anyone could beat you. So her doing it doesn't exactly add up to an Olympic future. If she brings it up at tea, I shall put it into the category of ordinary, common or garden boasting, and I shall say 'Pooh!' accordingly."

"Not her speciality, of course, swimming," said Jack glumly. "I was thinking of trying to make it mine, but I shan't now."

"Well, I wouldn't, either," agreed Uncle Parker. "If old Rosie's already got a head start on you, not much future there."

"So what *shall* I have as a speciality?"

Jack did not really believe Uncle Parker would be able to answer this question. Hours of solitary, nail-biting thought on his own part had as yet produced no result.

"I'll think about it," promised Uncle Parker. "Think about it and let you know."

"Thanks. Nothing to do with maths, thanks, and nothing

to do with sport. We've already got two walking computers, and Mother's always carping on about cleaning silver cups."

"Doesn't leave much," said Uncle Parker. "But I'll try. Hello. Here come the genii."

Jack turned his head and they both watched the advance of the Bagthorpes. You could hear them better than you could see them because they were bawling out a song together. It sounded like *Frère Jacques* but could easily have been something else. None of the Bagthorpes were great singers, though Rosie played the violin and Tess the oboe and piano and both were always appearing in concerts, and William (for his third String) was a wizard on the drums. Mr Bagthorpe was given to saying on occasion that William must have been a tribal warrior in a previous incarnation, which, while interesting, was hard on his present family.

They don't look like geniuses, Jack thought, not for the first time. *Just like anybody else's brother and sisters they look.*

Now William, lank and sandy, had Rosie on his shoulders, clutching and screaming as she swayed up there. Tess (who was thirteen and read Voltaire in the original for pleasure and was a Black Belt in Judo, besides talking like a dictionary) ran behind, beating William with a branch.

Normal, even, sometimes, thought Jack. He even knew that

they were all fond of him, in their own way. *But more as if I was a kind of pet, or something,* he thought. *As if I'm just* harmless. *Not as an equal. I want to be equal.*

Now they were through the wicket between garden and meadow and William finally pitched the shrieking Rosie somersaulting on to the grass.

"Didn't hurt yourself, did you, Jacko?" William pitched himself full length beside him. For answer, Jack raised his skinned elbows.

"Making a grand exit," said Tess. "Gosh, they look sore."

"Hey – Uncle Park!" Rosie was up again now. "Guess what? I beat Jack doing ten lengths."

"Pooh!" Uncle Parker was true to his word.

"What d'you mean, 'Pooh'?" demanded Rosie. "He's three years older than me."

"And swims like an elephant," returned Uncle Parker, admittedly unflatteringly. "There's too much boasting goes on at this house."

"Not boasting," corrected Tess. "Mother and Father both say we should be proud of achievement. They say it's an inbred fault of the English to underestimate themselves. Their favourite sin is 'pride that apes humility'."

"Well, if it is," said Uncle Parker, "you lot are certainly doing your bit to redress the balance. Enough boasting here to leaven the whole loaf."

"Except for me," said Jack, "who hasn't got anything to boast about."

"Never mind," Tess said. "I bet you've got a hidden talent that will emerge. Einstein was a terribly late starter, you know, prodigiously late. You've got to have got some hidden talent somewhere or you couldn't be a Bagthorpe. You might go to the moon when you grow up, or anything."

"I don't particularly want to go to the moon, thank you," Jack said. "Any fool could go there."

"Anonymous from Grimsby reckons there's an alien intelligence out there," William told them. "Says he keeps picking up signals from outer space."

"What do they say?" demanded Jack, interested.

William stood up.

"Sorry. I told you – a veil of secrecy must be preserved. I think I'll go and see if he's there now, actually. Might've got something new."

Jack watched him go.

One day I will punch him when he says that, he thought.

"Better get back myself." Tess stood up now. "I want to finish my Voltaire. And you'd better finish that Birthday Portrait of Grandma –" this to Rosie. (Rosie's second string was portraits.)

When they had all gone Jack lay back on the warm

grass and shut his eyes. He decided to try to go into a trance and get some inspiration that way, since ordinary straightforward thinking never got him anywhere. Uncle Parker, however, evidently misinterpreted this action.

"No good just lying back and giving up, you know."

"I haven't given up. I'm trying to go into a trance."

"Hmmmmmm."

There was silence for a while. Jack became conscious of the nearby humming of bees and flies, and the effect was hypnotic and he really did begin to think he was on the verge of a trance when Uncle Parker shouted, "I've got it!"

Jack shot up as if stung. His head went fizzy and black.

"You have?" He was still half hypnotised.

"I most certainly have."

"Jack! Russell! Tea!"

He turned. His mother was standing by the rose arch, waving.

"Damn," he said. "How long was I in a trance?"

"In a *trance*? You, young Jack, were in a trance my elbow," said Uncle Parker severely. "Asleep, that's what you were. There's got to be a bit of diligence and application if we're going to do anything with you, I can see that. Coming, Laura!"

He unfolded himself from the deckchair, all six foot four of him, and looked down at Jack.

"You may as well come and have some tea," he said. "Get some energy up. You're going to need it."

Jack scrambled up and hurried to keep pace with him.

"It's nothing sporting, is it?" he asked. "I said not sporting."

"It's not sport. How old did we say the old lady was?"

"Seventy-five," Jack told him. "And Grandpa's eighty-five. Not today, though. I hope I don't get as deaf as that when I'm old."

"Your grandfather," said Uncle Parker, "is not as deaf as you all fear. He's what I call SD – and you can be that at any age."

"What's SD? Stone Deaf?"

"Selectively Deaf. You hear, in effect, just as much as you wish to hear. And I am bound to say that if I were married to a lady who talks like your grandmother does, *I* should be SD – very much so."

"I don't think you ought to say that, on her birthday," said Jack. "I mean, I know what you mean, but it's not very kind to say it. Not on her birthday."

"Sorry. No offence."

They trudged companionably up the terrace steps and went through the French windows and into the Birthday Party.

Grandma was sitting at the far end of the table, though

all that was visible was the odd wisp of white hair, because she was behind a large cake on a high stand. The cake was forested with candles. Jack had no intention of counting them. He knew for a fact that there would be seventy-five. His mother did not believe in doing things by halves. She would light the candles when the time came, and the icing would start melting while she was halfway through and by the time all the candles were lit the icing would be hopelessly larded with multicoloured grease and the whole top slice of the cake would have to be cut off and thrown to the birds. It happened every year. Mr Bagthorpe thought the practice dangerous and unnecessary, and said so, but was ignored. He even said that the birds ought to be protected, but no one took any notice of that either – least of all the birds, who sorted the crumbs with lightning dexterity and left the greased icing to seep, in the course of time and nature, into the lawn, with no apparent detriment to the daisies.

"Hello, Grandma," said Jack. "Happy Birthday."

He went down the table past the bristling cake and kissed her. Her skin was very soft and powdery and smelled unaccountably of warm pear drops.

"You are a good boy," said Grandma.

"What about me?" enquired Uncle Parker, delivering his own peck.

"I know perfectly well who you are," said Grandma. "You are that good-for-nothing young man who married Celia and ran Thomas over." (Thomas was an ill-favoured and cantankerous ginger tom who had unfortunately got in the way of Uncle Parker's car some five years previously, and whom Grandma had martyred to the point where one always half expected her to refer to him as "St Thomas".)

"That's me," said Uncle Parker mildly. "Sorry about that, Grandma. Nice old cat that was. Just not very nippy on his feet."

"He was a jewel," said Grandma. "He was given me on my fourth birthday, and I was devoted to him."

No one contradicted her. Clearly, no ginger tom in history had ever survived sixty odd years, with or without the intervention of Uncle Parker's deplorable driving. But today was Grandma's birthday and she was not to be contradicted. (She was rarely contradicted anyway. It was a whole lot of trouble to contradict Grandma. If Grandma said seven sixes were fifty-two, you agreed with her, as a rule. The odds against convincing her otherwise were practically a million to one anyway, and life was too short.)

"He was a jewel." Grandma repeated her observation a trifle argumentatively. Grandma liked arguments and got disappointed when nobody else wanted them.

"*You're* a jewel," said Mr Bagthorpe diplomatically. He

dropped a kiss on her head and pulled out a chair for his wife and the danger was temporarily averted.

Jack, seated between Uncle Parker and Rosie, cast a speculative eye over the table. All the customary Bagthorpe birthday trimmings were present, he noted with satisfaction. The sausage rolls (hot), salmon and cucumber sandwiches, asparagus rolls, stuffed eggs, cream meringues, chocolate truffle cake and Mrs Fosdyke's Special Trifle – all were there, and the eyes of all Bagthorpes present were riveted upon them. There was a pause. Jack's eyes moved to the top of the table. Grandma, thwarted of her argument, was hanging fire on purpose, he guessed, to pay them back. They waited.

"For what we are about to receive," she eventually remarked, eyes piously closed, "may the Lord make us truly thankful."

On the last two words her eyes blinked open like a cobra's and a hand went rapidly out to the nearest pile of stuffed eggs.

"Amen," gabbled the company, with the exception of Uncle Parker who said loudly and cheerfully, "Hear, hear!"

The food began to vanish at an astonishing rate.

"Well, darlings," said Mrs Bagthorpe. "What is there to tell?"

Babel was instantly let loose as all present with the

exception of Grandpa, Uncle Parker and Jack, began to talk with their mouths full. Mrs Bagthorpe believed that meals should be civilised occasions with a brisk and original interchange of views and ideas, but as none of the younger Bagthorpes were prepared to talk at the cost of stuffing themselves, they invariably did both at the same time.

"I beathja teleths," came a crumb-choked voice by Jack's elbow.

"Told you," said Jack to Uncle Parker.

"What was that, Rosie?" enquired Mrs Bagthorpe. "You left what in the bath?"

"I beat Jack doing ten lengths." This time Rosie's voice was shamingly distinct and, what was worse, fell into a rare lull in the general din.

"Did you *really*?" exclaimed Mrs Bagthorpe, and "Pooh!" said Uncle Parker simultaneously with such force that morsels of crust flew across the table at his wife.

Conversation ceased abruptly.

"Did you say something, Russell?" asked Mrs Bagthorpe.

"I said 'Pooh!'"

"That's what he said before when I told him," squeaked Rosie indignantly. "And it's good – it is! Jack's three years older than me and I beat him and it *is* good!"

"Of course it is, darling," agreed her mother. "And I'm terribly proud of you. Bad luck, Jack."

"Bad luck Jack my foot, leg and elbow," said Uncle Parker. Everyone stared at him except Grandpa who was being SD and evidently did not realise what he was about to miss.

"I'll elaborate," said Uncle Parker. "In my opinion young Jack here, while being a perfectly good chap and worth ten of most here present, swims with the approximate grace and agility of an elephant."

No one contradicted him.

"The fact, therefore," he continued, "that young Rosie here, while also being perfectly acceptable in many ways though some might say too clever by half, the fact that she has beaten Jack doing ten lengths seems to me to be an event totally devoid of interest. It seems, in fact, to be a non-event of the first order."

"I am three years younger," piped Rosie.

Uncle Parker turned to her.

"Kindly do not tell me that again," he told her. "I have been given that information at least three times in the last hour and am by now in perfect possession of it."

"No, Uncle Parker," said Rosie meekly. "I mean, yes."

"Crikey, Uncle P," said William, "you are in a lather. Anyone'd think Rosie'd beaten *you*."

"I don't doubt that she could," returned Uncle Parker calmly. "I am a notoriously bad swimmer, and I dislike getting wet unnecessarily. The only good reason for swimming, so far as I can see, is to escape drowning."

"The thing I best remember about that jewel of a cat," said Grandma reminiscently, "was his extraordinary sweetness of nature. He hadn't a streak of malice in him."

It was, after all, Grandma's Birthday Party, and she probably felt she was losing her grip on it.

"That cat," said Mr Bagthorpe, caught off-guard and swallowing the bait, "was the most cross-grained evil-eyed thing that ever went on four legs. If I had a pound note for every time that animal bit me, I should be a rich man, now."

"How *can* you, Henry!" cried Grandma, delighted that things were warming up.

"I'd be Croesus," said Mr Bagthorpe relentlessly. "Midas. Paul Getty. That cat bit people like he was being paid for it in kippers."

"There he would lie, hour upon hour, with his great golden head nestled in my lap," crooned Grandma, getting into her stride, "and I would feel the sweetness flowing out of him. When I lost Thomas, something irreplaceable went out of my life."

"Bilge, Mother," said Mr Bagthorpe. "That cat was nothing short of diabolical. He was a legend. He was feared and hated for miles around. In fact I clearly remember that the first dawnings of respect I ever felt for Russell here began on the day he ran the blasted animal over."

"Language, dear," murmured Mrs Bagthorpe automatically.

"Not on purpose, of course," said Uncle Parker.

"Of course not on purpose!" snapped Mr Bagthorpe. "The way you drive, you couldn't hit a brick wall, let alone a cat."

"It just wasn't very nippy on its toes, you see," said Uncle Parker apologetically to Grandma.

"It nipped me on *my* toes," said William. "Bags of times."

The rest turned unsmilingly towards him.

"All right," he said. "So it wasn't all that funny. But what about this 'Pooh!' business of Uncle P's? Let's get back to that. Unless you want to hear what Anonymous from Grimsby told me."

"I don't think you'd better," said Jack. "It'd be breaking the veil of secrecy."

He enjoyed making this remark, but his pleasure was short-lived.

"I wish you'd learn to use words accurately," said Mr Bagthorpe testily. (He wrote scripts for television and now and again got obsessed about words, which in his darker moments he believed would eventually become extinct, probably in his own lifetime.) "You can't break a veil. A veil, by its very nature, is of a fine-spun, almost transparent texture, and while it may be *rent*, or even—"

"For crying out *loud*," said Uncle Parker.

"Oh, dearest," murmured his wife, "must you...?"

This was the first time Aunt Celia had spoken. She had not even noticed when Uncle Parker had sprayed crumbs at her. The reason for this was that she was gazing at a large piece of bark by her plate. No one had remarked on this because Aunt Celia often brought pieces of bark, ivy or stone (and even, on one memorable occasion, a live snail) to table to gaze on as she ate, even at other people's parties. She did this because she said it inspired her. It was partly to do with her pot-throwing, she said, and partly her poetry. There was no argument about this since her poetry and pottery alike were not much understood by the other Bagthorpes. They respected it without knowing what on earth it was all about. Also, Aunt Celia was very beautiful – like a naiad, Uncle Parker would fondly tell people – and looked even more so when she was being wistful and faraway. In the hurly-burly of Bagthorpe mealtimes she was looked upon more as an ornament than a participant.

She had, however, now spoken, and the Bagthorpes were sufficiently surprised by this to fall silent again.

"Must I what, dearest?" asked Uncle Parker, leaning forward.

"I was just on the verge... I thought... I was almost..."

Her voice trailed off. When Aunt Celia did speak it was usually like this, in a kind of shorthand. She started sentences and left you to guess the ends – if, of course, you thought it worth your while. By and large, the Bagthorpes did not. Uncle Parker, however, did.

"Just on the verge of...?" he prompted delicately.

"What about my portrait?" demanded Rosie loudly. Having had her swimming feat passed over as a mere nothing, she had no intention of letting her Birthday Portrait go the same way. It was set on an easel just by Grandma herself and no one had commented on it because in the first place they were currently more interested in food, and in the second because it looked unfinished.

"Where's her mouth?" demanded Tess.

"And her nose?" asked Jack.

"Not to mention her eyes," added William. "*Might* come out right, Rosie, but doesn't look like one of your best. You've got her ears wrong. You've got 'em too flat. Look – you look – they stick out a lot more than you've got them."

The entire table turned its eyes on Grandma's ears. Grandma looked frostily back at them.

"My ears," she stated, "are one of my best features. This was one of Alfred's favourite contentions during our courtship. "I could love you for your ears alone," he would say, and, 'Grace, your ears are like petals, veritable petals.' Isn't that so?"

All eyes now turned towards Grandpa who was stolidly making his way through what was probably his tenth stuffed egg. In his rare communicative moments he would sometimes confide that one of the few pleasures left to him in life was stuffed eggs – that and skewering wasps he would say – and the latter was unfortunately seasonal. (A relative of Grandpa's had once died of a wasp sting and he was convinced that this would be the way he would go too, unless it were under the wheels of Uncle Parker's car.)

"Alfred!"

Grandma leaned forward and jabbed at his arm, determined that he should give testimony. He dropped his egg and blinked blankly at her.

"Eh? Eh? Happy Birthday, my dear."

"SD," murmured Uncle Parker to Jack. "See what I mean?"

"I was saying about my *ears*!" Grandma pointed to her own with either hand simultaneously, thereby taking on a distinctly lunatic look.

"Ah – my ears!" Grandpa sounded relieved. He picked up his egg and started in on it again. "Aid's playing up a bit. One of those days. I don't reckon much to these aids. It's the weather, you know. They're affected by the weather."

"*My* ears!" Grandma positively shrieked. Grandpa did not turn a hair. He did not even seem to know she had spoken. He simply went on polishing off his stuffed egg. He had flecks of yolk in his beard, Jack noticed.

"The candles!" cried Mrs Bagthorpe with tremendous gaiety. She rose and swept theatrically towards the head of the table where Grandma sat fuming behind her porcupine of a cake.

"I hope you're satisfied!" she hissed at Mr Bagthorpe as she passed behind him.

He turned to Uncle Parker for support.

"I never said a word about her ears," he protested. "I may have said one or two rather strong things about that blood-crazed animal of—"

"Ssssh!" Mrs Bagthorpe had just struck her first match and her hiss blew it out. She struck another.

"The older you get," observed Grandma dismally, "the more you are trodden down. Life is nothing but a process of being trodden down from the cradle to the grave."

"Note the change of tactics," said Uncle Parker to Jack *sotto voce*. "She's not half bad, I'll say that."

Mrs Bagthorpe was now lighting candles with practised rapidity and had signalled Tess to start on the other side of the cake. Grandma kept up a muttered monologue as the conflagration spread before her. Jack could not catch all of it but it seemed mostly to be about graves, and ingratitude.

"The crackers!" exclaimed Mr Bagthorpe suddenly. He was evidently remorseful and felt bound to do his own share of drumming up a festive air. "By Jove – can't have the cake cut without hats on!"

"Where *are* the crackers?" asked William.

They looked about the littered table.

"I put them out – I did! There was one on every side plate!" Tess was frantically darting her hands among the candles as she spoke. "And Daisy helped me."

There was a real silence now.

"Good God," said Uncle Parker at last. He had gone quite white. "Daisy."

"She's not here," said Jack unnecessarily.

"Daisy, Daisy, where – oh where—" moaned Aunt Celia wildly. She pushed away her piece of bark and stood swaying like a reed.

"I clean forgot. Oh my God. I'll find her – I will!"

"But what – where – the lake…" moaned Aunt Celia.

At Grandma's end of the table concern for Daisy was not half so strong as concern for the crackers.

"She was *here*, I tell you, putting out crackers." Tess's face was lit now from below, the cake was sputtering and ablaze.

"We'll have to blow the candles – we'll have to sing – we can't wait!" shrieked Mrs Bagthorpe.

"Look – here's one!" Mr Bagthorpe snatched a cracker from under a crumpled napkin. "Quick – Jack – you pull it with me, and then there'll be a hat for Grandma."

Jack reached over and they pulled hard. *Crack!*

Chapter Two

WHAT HAPPENED NEXT was so confusing that even when you put together the different accounts of everyone there present, nothing like a clear picture ever emerged. The Fire Brigade, when they arrived, could certainly make neither head nor tail of it and had never before attended a fire like it.

In the Bagthorpe family, the incident became known, in course of time, as "The Day Zero Piddled While Home Burned". (No one actually saw this, but he sometimes did when he got nervous, and it rhymed so well with 'fiddled' that it was passed as Poetic Licence.)

Only a handful of facts – as opposed to impressions, which were legion – emerged. These were as follows:

Fact the First

Daisy, aged four, had been sitting underneath the table the whole time the party was going on.

Fact the Second

What she had been doing under the table was opening all the crackers and taking out whatever was inside. (After the fire quite a lot of melted plastic was found mixed in with the carpet.)

Fact the Third

What was also under the table (mistaken by Daisy for a second box of crackers) was a large box of fireworks which were a surprise present to Grandma from Uncle Parker. He said afterwards he had given them in the hope they would liven things up.

Fact the Fourth

Daisy was in the company of a mongrel dog called Zero who belonged to the Bagthorpes in general and Jack in particular. He had just appeared one day in the garden, and stayed. The Bagthorpes had advertised him in the local paper, but nobody seemed to have recognised the description, or if they had, had not come forward. Mr Bagthorpe disassociated himself from Zero and would often pretend he had never set eyes on him.

"There's a dog out there on the landing," he would say. "A great pudding-footed thing covered in fur. See what it wants."

It was Mr Bagthorpe who had given Zero his name.

"If there was anything less than nothing," he had said, "that hound would be it. But there isn't, so we'll have to settle for Zero."

The family computers, William and Rosie, had pointed out that mathematically speaking there was a whole lot to choose from that was less than zero, but Mr Bagthorpe had dismissed this as idle speculation.

"You show me something less than nothing, and I'll believe you," he had told them.

Mr Bagthorpe could be very categorical, and was especially so on subjects about which he knew practically nothing, like mathematics. Anyway, Zero was called that, and Jack sometimes used to wonder if it had affected him, and given him an inferiority complex, because sometimes Zero seemed to drag his feet about rather, and his ears looked droopier than when they had first had him. Jack would spend hours poring over old snapshots of Zero, comparing ears. When they were alone together Jack would praise Zero up and tell him how wonderful and intelligent he was, to try and counteract this. Also, when in public Jack would call him "Nero" so as to give him a bit of dignity in the eyes of others, and as Zero hardly ever came when he was called anyway, it didn't make much difference.

So the fact was that Zero was under the table with Daisy, who had probably given him some food to keep him quiet. When she was cross-examined afterwards Daisy said she had taken him under the table with her because she had thought it would be lonely under there by herself. Mr Bagthorpe flatly refused to believe this, and said that Daisy must have plotted the whole thing because if Zero hadn't been there with her none of the things that did happen would have happened.

He and Uncle Parker used to have rows about this for weeks afterwards. Uncle Parker would say that while he admitted that Daisy was a genius (she had to be, with a reading age of 7.4 and the way she was always writing her thoughts on walls, and what with having Aunt Celia for a mother) she was too young to have plotted anything as complicated as that. He would also point out that the whole thing had hinged not so much on Zero being under the table as on the moment when a certain cracker was pulled, Mr Bagthorpe being the person who had made this suggestion and connived at its execution. Mr Bagthorpe would retaliate by saying that the coincidence of Uncle Parker's having bought a large box of fireworks, and of Uncle Parker's daughter being under the table with them, might strike some people as rather more than coincidence. He would usually end up advising Uncle Parker to take himself and Daisy off to a psychiatrist.

Fact the Fifth

When Jack and Mr Bagthorpe pulled the single available cracker, Zero, who was probably already nervous at being trapped so long under a table surrounded by so many feet and legs, had blown his mind. He had sprung forward, got both sets of paws wound in the tablecloth and pulled the whole lot after him, including the cake.

At the actual moment this happened, of course, no one had any inkling that Zero had been under the table, and the sight of the tablecloth leaping forward and rolling about on the floor had almost unhinged some of them, notably Grandma, Mrs Bagthorpe and Aunt Celia. The latter certainly always referred to it afterwards as a "manifestation" and would refer to how Daisy had been "delivered". (This also helped make Daisy seem less of a culprit, because it made her seem more a victim, and it was difficult to see her in both roles at once.)

Grandma herself, with it being her birthday and her cake, had taken the whole thing personally and had thought she was being struck by a thunderbolt. She had miraculously escaped injury altogether, but Rosie's Birthday Portrait had been one of the first things to go up in flames and always afterwards Grandma saw this as what she called a "Sign". A Sign of what she didn't specify, but she always said it very darkly, and when she was feeling low. Sometimes the others, to cheer her up when she got brooding about it, would say that if it were a "Sign" it was clearly a Sign that Rosie's Birthday Portrait had not been worth a light – so to speak.

Grandpa had not of course heard the whole lot of cracks and bangs as all the crackers Daisy had dismantled started going off, but had not failed to note that the last remaining stuffed egg had been suddenly snatched from under his very nose. He had risen hastily to grab after it, knocked over his own chair, tripped, and fallen over Grandma and lost his hearing aid.

When the firemen came they were very helpful and said they would keep an eye open for it, but what with the whole room by then ablaze and the curtains just beginning to catch fire, they didn't really have time. They were very good firemen but they did seem nervous about bangers still going off and sudden flares of blue or green light. They definitely seemed jumpy. Afterwards, when they were having some beer with the Bagthorpes to moisten their dried-out mouths, they apologised for this. They said that the Bagthorpe fire was not really a run-of-the-mill job or something for which they had been properly prepared during their training.

They stayed on quite a while after the fire was out. They sat round in the kitchen and told the Bagthorpes a lot of interesting things about arson and so on, and before they left Rosie got all their autographs. They seemed quite flattered by this. Rosie told them the autographs were more of a gamble than anything, just in case one of them ever died rescuing someone from a burning building, and became a national hero and got a post-mortem award on the television. Soon after this the firemen left.

When they had gone, Mrs Fosdyke (who came in daily to do for the Bagthorpes, but refused to sleep in) said she thought they had all looked too young and inexperienced to be proper firemen. She did not believe they had been a proper Fire Brigade at all, and said that her carpet and her furniture would not now be in the state they were in if a proper Brigade had been sent in time. People were too easily deceived by uniforms, she said. (Mrs Fosdyke had missed the actual moment when the tablecloth went up in the air and was naturally bitter about this.)

Nobody did anything about cleaning up after the fire that night. They all sat round and talked about it till quite late. At around ten o'clock Mr Bagthorpe went out to close his greenhouse for the night and fell over Zero, who had not been seen since the Party. Jack had even feared him lost, and had had a quick look among the debris for signs of bones, though he was not certain what exactly a burned bone would look like.

"That infernal hound's back," Mr Bagthorpe announced and Zero crept in behind him. He was still shaking. Jack stood up.

"I'm going to bed," he said. Zero always slept in his room and he looked as if he needed a rest.

"Nobody's sung 'Happy Birthday' to me yet," Grandma said. "My birthday's nearly over. I shan't be having many more. I suppose it doesn't really matter. Nothing really matters."

"Oh, darling, of *course* it matters. We'll all sing it now, this very moment, won't we, everyone?" cried Mrs Bagthorpe. "But what a shame about the candles."

Chapter Three

JACK WONDERED WHETHER Zero's legs looked wobbly because of the chilliness or because they had still not picked up after last night. Zero had certainly not wanted to go with Jack when he went to have a look at the scene of the disaster in daylight, or rather, dawnlight. It was not yet six o'clock. The gutted and blackened state of the dining-room had shaken Jack himself. The tattered curtains swung to and fro in the shattered windows. It looked more like a scene out of a film than home.

Jack and Zero were padding together over the fields towards The Knoll, Uncle Parker's house. (He had wanted to call it "Parker Knoll" but Aunt Celia had said she would leave him if he did.) Jack had not slept too well.

He had not been thinking especially about the fire, though he had once or twice been tempted to go down and make sure that there wasn't anything still smouldering. Mrs Fosdyke had been very definite about the dubious credentials of the firemen who had come, and they had certainly been jumpy. But what was really exercising his mind was Uncle Parker's idea. He had obviously thought of a way that he, Jack, could become immortal and keep up with the rest of the Bagthorpes. He had been, maddeningly, on the very brink of imparting it on the previous afternoon.

"If I get immortal, old chap," Jack told Zero now, "I'll make sure you do as well. I'll work you in on the act somehow."

He made quite a few other similarly encouraging remarks to Zero on the walk, because his self-confidence must have suffered a severe setback last night, and Mr Bagthorpe, for one, wouldn't let him forget it in a hurry. (Jack was right about this. Quite often in weeks and even months to come he would say things like, "Look to yourself – here comes that incendiary hound again," or, "If that animal's stopping, the house insurance'll have to go up again, you realise that".)

Jack was going to The Knoll so early partly because he was impatient to hear the idea and partly because he knew that this was Uncle Parker's best time of the day.

Uncle Parker spent his whole time apparently lounging around and led a life of ease, but he had long ago confided to Jack that this sort of thing was by no means as simple as it looked. He rose at six, summer and winter alike, did a workout and then jogged for three miles round the fields. He then went home, took a cold shower, prepared orange juice, toast and coffee and retired into his study with the morning papers, which he paid an extra fifty pence a week to have delivered early. What he did then, or so Jack gathered, was something to do with stocks and shares. In the village opinion ranged from suspecting him of being the compiler of *The Times* crossword (which would explain why Aunt Celia was so good at it) to his being an Enemy Agent (this by people who had had particularly narrow escapes from Uncle Parker's car). He stayed in the study till about ten answering letters and making telephone calls, and then the rest of the day was free.

This infuriated other people who were mystified as to what Uncle Parker actually did in life to maintain, for instance, the kind of car he drove round in, terrifying the life out of everyone else. They were also irritated by the way he looked so lean and fit while apparently inviting flab and liver trouble by lounging around sipping gin and doing crosswords.

"I *am* an idle devil," Uncle Parker once told Jack. "But at least I work at it."

Jack could see him now, at a distance, clad only in shorts and vest, jogging along in a shower of spray. He shouted and Uncle Parker waved and veered in his direction.

"Up early," he called. "House hasn't gone up again, has it?"

"They're all asleep. I couldn't sleep."

"I'll tell you what," said Uncle Parker, drawing up to him. "No more could I. And the thing that kept coming at me all night was those allfired mottoes."

"Mottoes?"

"In all those crackers. We'll never know what they were, now. I use 'em, you know, at dinner parties, as conversation-stoppers. The minute they start on about politics, out I come with one of my little mottoes. To tell you the truth, I collect them. Got a little book full of 'em. I wonder who thinks them up."

"Nobody, I don't suppose," Jack said. "I should think they're handed down through the generations. They're immortal. And that reminds me…"

"I know, I know." Uncle Parker raised a silencing hand. "You jog along back with me, and I'll tell all."

"I don't know if Zero's up to jogging." Jack eyed him dubiously. "Do his ears look droopy to you?"

"He's not much of a livewire at the best of times." Uncle

Parker in turn surveyed him. "On the other hand, he did have a bit of a raw deal yesterday. If he had any spirit, he'd take a piece out of Daisy's leg."

"He'd never!" Jack was shocked.

"To be frank –" Uncle Parker started jogging and Jack kept up – "I was about ready to take a piece out of her leg myself. All those mottoes!"

"What about being immortal, then?" Uncle Parker would keep going off on different tacks if he were not pinned down.

"Ah. Well. What I've hatched up for you, young Jack, is going to shake that family of yours to its foundations. To its core."

"It is?"

"What you are going to be," Uncle Parker told him, as they entered the field that was the home straight to The Knoll, "is a prophet."

Jack was struggling to keep up. He was a full foot shorter than Uncle Parker and what was a jog to him was an all-out striding for Jack.

"You mean—?" He was bewildered. "Make a profit? Be in business? But I said nothing to *do* with figures."

Uncle Parker stopped so suddenly that Jack was several yards past him before he realised, and had to turn back.

"What I mean," he said, "is that you are to become a

mystery, an enigma, a mystically gifted being beyond all ken. Beyond anybody's ken."

There was quite a long silence then, which allowed Zero to catch up.

"It was what you said yourself, yesterday," Uncle Parker said. "About going into a trance."

"Oh, I wasn't in a real one," Jack assured him hastily. "All I meant—"

"I *know* you weren't in a real one," said Uncle Parker. "But what if you had been?"

They looked at one another.

"What," said Uncle Parker pregnantly, "if you'd been having a *Vision*?"

"B-but I never do have visions. I've never had one in my whole life. I—"

"From now on," Uncle Parker told him firmly, "you will have Visions. Frequently. You will also hear Voices."

"W-will I?"

"You will receive," said Uncle Parker, "Messages."

"But I don't get them either."

"Didn't," corrected Uncle Parker. "You *didn't* get Messages. From now on, you will get them. Daily. Well, no, perhaps not daily, not at the start. If we overdo things, it'll arouse suspicions. No, to begin with, you will just get the odd Message."

"What sort of Message?"

Uncle Parker was not even listening.

"And hear the odd Voice. But there again, we don't want to go overdoing the Joan of Arc bit, not at the beginning."

"Look, Uncle Parker. I know you're trying to help. But—"

"I've got the first move all planned. As soon as I get back and change, I'll prime you up. But you realise –" he started jogging again, and Jack had no option but to follow suit – "that there'll have to be a bit of discipline and hard work."

"Well, yes, but—"

"I've told you. The easier it looks, the harder it is. And to start with, I think you ought to start practising a few basic skills."

Jack did not bother to ask what these basic skills were because he knew he was about to hear anyway.

"One that occurred to me last night when I was lying there thinking about those cursed mottoes, was water divining. Dowsing. Read an article about that only last week, and there's definitely something in it. Might even give it a go myself. Just think – you and me waltzing about the place with forked twigs leaping in our hands like live fish – give 'em something to think about that will!"

Jack felt, despite himself, the stirrings of excitement. He

too had read about water divining, but had imagined that you had to be the seventh son of a seventh son even to think of taking it up. He said so.

"Pooh!" returned Uncle Parker. "Anyone can do it. Just takes a bit of application. Or else," he added, "a map showing local underground water courses."

"You mean…?"

"I mean," said Uncle Parker, "that we shall both have a good stab at making ourselves into diviners of water. But if all else fails, we shall content ourselves with convincing other people that you, at any rate, are."

"Oh," said Jack. "Cheating."

"Being one cleverer than they are," corrected Uncle Parker. "Isn't that what it's all about?"

"Well, I suppose…"

"Come on, old son, brace up." They were entering the garden of The Knoll now. "You stop here, and I'll be back in a jiffy and let you have the lowdown on the whole thing."

He jogged off over the lawn leaving his footprints in the dew.

"You could try having a ferret round for a dowsing twig," he called over his shoulder. "Hazel's best."

Jack took a look about, but Uncle Parker's garden was full of flowering shrubs and rambling roses and did not look half wild enough to house dowsing twigs. After a while he gave up looking, and sat on a stone bench and got Zero to sit in front of him while he took a good look at his ears. He was not really satisfied with what he saw, so he spent the time waiting for Uncle Parker to reappear in giving Zero a pep talk. He told him how the whole thing had been Daisy's fault, how sensible Zero had been to clear right off out of things instead of hanging around waiting to be burned, and how Grandma had said that the carpet and curtains were getting shabby anyway.

"By the time the Insurance have paid up," he told Zero, "our whole dining-room'll be better than it's ever been. And it's all due to you. Good boy. Good *boy*."

He leaned back to survey Zero's ears and assess how much good his pep talk had done, but just then Uncle Parker came back. He sat next to Jack and produced two loose-leaf notebooks. He passed one to Jack.

"Here," he said. "Guard this with your life."

Interested, Jack opened it.

"But there's nothing in it!"

"Yet," said Uncle Parker. "There will be. This is for notes and records of the Campaign. Better not to have one, of course, better to commit all to memory – but there you are. With due respect, I don't think you've got the memory."

"No." Jack was not offended. He was used to this kind of remark.

"Now, here's a pen." Uncle Parker passed one over, the felt-tipped variety. He opened his own notebook and Jack saw that his first page was already full.

"Write down 'Create Mysterious Impression'," commanded Uncle Parker. "And underline it."

Jack obeyed.

"One 'e' in mysterious and two 'esses' in impression," said Uncle Parker, "but never mind."

"What does it *mean*?" Jack asked.

"It means," Uncle Parker told him, "that from now on you are to behave, now and then, Mysteriously. What I mean by this is that you are to give the impression, now and again, that your eyes are fixed on things invisible to mortal eyes. That you are, possibly, seeing Visions."

"How?" Jack asked.

"Watch me."

Uncle Parker laid aside his notebook and looked with a kind of mad intensity at something just to the right of Jack's head. It was as if he were trying to look Jack in the eyes to hypnotise him, but missing. His look deepened in such a definite way that Jack, alarmed, actually turned his head to see if there were anything there behind him.

"Aha!" Uncle Parker was triumphant. "Ha! Got you!

See what I mean? That's the kind of look to give 'em! Come on, you do it. Have a go at looking Mysterious."

Jack, whose sole dramatic experience to date had been playing Third Shepherd in a Nativity play when he was six, tried to oblige. He fixed his gaze on a point behind Uncle Parker's left ear and tried to imagine he was seeing a Vision. He kept it up for what seemed a very long time. He tried not to blink because that seemed a good and visionary thing to do, but then his eyes started to water and he ended up having to blink twice as much as usual. Through a blur he moved his gaze on to Uncle Parker.

"Look," said Uncle Parker kindly, "it was a good start. Fine. But you did look a bit as if rigor mortis had set in. The whole idea is to look Mysterious and faraway – there was too much *stare* about the whole thing. Now watch me again."

Jack watched Uncle Parker do it and then Uncle Parker watched him have another go. This time Jack decided on imagining a plateful of bacon, egg, sausage, tomato, mushroom and fried bread behind Uncle Parker's ear.

"How was that?" he asked, reluctantly letting the picture go.

"Better." Uncle Parker was emphatic. "Not far off first class. There was a whole lot of soul about that. You really looked as if you were seeing a Vision that time."

"I was," said Jack simply.

"We'll forget that for now," said Uncle Parker, "and get on to the first Vision."

"I thought that was it," said Jack.

"That," explained Uncle Parker, "was for you to go round doing a few times during the day. Do it while several people are around, if you can, and do it about twice this morning and the same this afternoon. Make sure they get the message."

"The awful thing would be if I laughed," Jack said.

"If you laugh," said Uncle Parker sternly, "I wash my hands of you. Clear?"

"Clear," Jack said. "There is one thing. Could Zero be in on it as well?"

Uncle Parker, floored, looked at Zero lying slumped by Jack's feet as if he were sculpted in dough.

"Now listen," he said, "I'll take you on, because by and large I think you're promising material. I think I'll make something of you. But that hound's another matter."

"Don't call him an h-o-u-n-d," pleaded Jack. He spelled the word out because he was pretty sure that Zero, being so simple in other ways, would almost certainly not understand. "Please. Father does it all the time. It undermines his confidence. And he's in a terrible state after last night."

"We're all in a terrible state after last night," said Uncle

Parker. "And some of us didn't do double somersaults with burning tablecloths on our heads."

"You would," said Jack, "if you'd been under there, in his position."

"We won't go into that," said Uncle Parker. "All I'm saying is that any question of that dog having Visions is out. Come to think –" he eyed Zero speculatively – "that's not quite right. Come to think, he goes round half the time looking as if he's having Visions. You could do worse than study him."

"Hear that?" Jack, delighted, bent and patted him. "Hear that, Zero? Good old boy!"

Zero wagged his tail lethargically.

"I'm glad you said that," Jack told Uncle Parker. "It's cheered him up no end."

"So – ready for another note." Uncle Parker changed the subject. "Write 'Vision One' and underline."

Jack obeyed.

"Now write what I dictate."

Jack poised his felt-tip ready.

"Write: 'I see… I see… I see a Lavender Man who Bears Tidings.'"

Jack let his pen drop.

"Write *what*?" he said incredulously.

"Never mind that. You write it down. 'I see dot dot

dot, I see dot dot dot, I see a Lavender Man who Bears Tidings.'"

Jack wrote it down in a fog.

"Now read it back to me."

Uncle Parker listened.

"You don't *say* dot dot dot," he explained patiently. "Those are to indicate pregnant pauses. I see… pause, I see… pause… Get it?"

"I get it." Jack altered his dot dot dots to '…'

"Now say it," ordered Uncle Parker. "With feeling."

Jack stood up.

"I don't think I want to go on with this," he said.

"Sit down," said Uncle Parker.

Jack sat down.

"I know. I know it's a damn-fool thing to say," Uncle Parker said.

"It certainly is," said Jack with feeling. "I can't say it. I've never said anything like it in my life."

"Precisely. You take the point exactly. You have never said anything like it in your life. And so when you do say it, around tea-time, after spending most of the day seeing Visions past people's ears, it's going to get noticed."

"It certainly is," said Jack again. "They'll probably send for the doctor."

"They won't," said Uncle Parker. "But if they do, make

sure you look past his ear as well. Do the Vision stuff on him like we practised. Might even help if they *do* call for a medical opinion."

"Actually," Jack said, "I think I might be going to go mad. What's it all about? What's all this about Lavender Men and Bearing?"

"Aha!" Uncle Parker was triumphant again. "*That's* where they start sitting up and taking notice. That's where I come in."

"It is?"

"Last week," explained Uncle Parker, "unbeknownst to your Aunt Celia, unbeknownst, in fact, to anyone in the world except myself, a tailor in the West End and possibly my bank manager, I purchased, after much deliberation, a lavender suit."

"A suit made of lavender?"

"A lavender-*coloured* suit, Jack, so far as I can describe it."

"Whatever for?"

"You're a bit young to understand," Uncle Parker told him. "I bought it because – I think because – I felt I wasn't quite living up to your Aunt Celia's ideal. I felt that if I took to wearing a lavender suit now and again, she would see in me the man she once hoped I was."

"Oh." Jack was as nonplussed as he had ever been in his life.

"Listen carefully. At around half-past six, I shall whip up your drive and emerge wearing the aforesaid lavender suit. I shall also bear tidings. I shall have, in other words, news for you."

"What news?"

"I don't think I should tell you that," said Uncle Parker. "If I do, I think it will be hard for you to act surprised when I tell you tonight, so it'll be better if you actually don't know. No offence. But you see what I mean."

"I wish I did," said Jack.

"Now look. It's all absolutely straightforward. You've got it all written down. One – you act Mysterious. Right?"

"Right."

"Two, you come out, round about tea-time, with Vision One. You say, 'I see dot dot dot I see dot dot dot et cetera.' Right?"

"I suppose so."

"That's it, then. That's all there is to it. Just leave the rest to me. By seven o'clock tonight, I promise you, you'll be Number One Attraction in the Bagthorpe ménage. Your wildest dream come true."

"Uncle Parker…"

"Well?"

"I think – yes, look! There is – there's smoke coming out of your house."

Uncle Parker turned towards The Knoll. From the window of one of the upper rooms was issuing, undeniably, a cloud of smoke.

"My God!" exclaimed Uncle Parker. "It's Daisy again!"

He leapt up and was off.

"You get back!" he shouted. "You get back and make out you've never set eyes on me since last night. Get back quick!"

He was running, not jogging.

"And act natural!" His parting words floated out as he disappeared into the smouldering Knoll.

"Come on, Zero."

Jack started off back home. It was still only just past seven. He stuffed the notebook deep in the pocket of his jeans.

"Act natural," he repeated to himself. Then, uncertainly, "Act Mysterious. Stage One, Act Mysterious."

It was all very confusing.

Chapter Four

THE FIRST THING Jack did when he got home was to get Vision One to materialise. He found all its ingredients except for the mushrooms, and set about frying them. No one else was down yet, but some of them were up because he could hear the far-off notes of an oboe and also from time to time a bump which was probably Mrs Bagthorpe unwinding herself from a Plough Posture. She had only recently taken up Yoga and was not very good at it but said she felt calmer already. She said she had felt calmer since the very first lesson when they had spent the whole hour just breathing. Jack had not noticed any real change. She certainly had not acted calm at Grandma's Birthday Party, he reflected. She had been in a fair lather even before the tablecloth took off.

He sat at the table with his fry-up and cut off all the bacon rinds to give Zero. He was just feeding them to him when the kitchen door opened and in came Mrs Fosdyke.

"Here!" she said sharply, without preliminaries. "No feeding at table. You know as well as I do."

"Sorry," he said. "I forgot."

"No one to see, you mean," returned Mrs Fosdyke. She had not stopped moving since she came in and had already removed her outer clothes to reveal a patterned wrap-round pinafore and exchanged her outdoor shoes for pink fur-edged slippers. (Mrs Fosdyke got cramps in her feet sometimes and the fur was a comfort, she said.)

"Your ma don't like you frying up," she observed. She went to the sink and set up a businesslike rattle.

"She likes you to get your vitamings of a morning. Grapefruit and that."

"I'll have a grapefruit as well," Jack offered.

"It's no good." Mrs Fosdyke withdrew her hands from the water and wiped them on her front. "I shall have to go and have a look. Never a wink did I have last night. It was as if all my furniture and ornaments was floating round me."

"I've seen it," he told her. "It's horrible. I shouldn't go. It'll only upset you."

It was too late. Mrs Fosdyke was halfw[illegible] before the words were out. Mrs Fosdyke was a very [illegible] mover. She moved like a hedgehog, Mr Bagthorpe was fond of saying, and was about as much use about the house. This was up to a point true. Mrs Fosdyke had to a fine art the ability to move around fast without actually doing very much. Mr Bagthorpe said a lot of people in the army had this gift, and in the Civil Service, but that it was rare in a Daily.

Mrs Fosdyke was uttering little shrieks and Jack, wiping his plate with a crust, could imagine her in there darting around on the sodden carpet. She came back in.

"Those beautiful chairs," she said. "Hairlooms. And all my best crystal. I could weep."

Her voice was actually quite choked and Jack delicately turned his eyes away while she blew into a tissue. A sudden thought struck him. *It might be a good idea*, he thought, *to practise giving a Mysterious Impression on her before any of the others got down*. Her eyes were not too good, and she would not be so likely to notice any flaws in his performance.

What I'll do, he thought, *next time she asks me something, I won't answer. Then she'll look at me to see what's the matter and I'll do the Mysterious Impression. I won't see bacon and eggs past her left ear, I've just had them. I'll see dinner*

reacle tart. Something like

that visions of food were going to quired soulful look better than anything

That dog, if it was mine, I'd take a slipper to," Mrs Fosdyke said. "And that Daisy the same. Little madam her."

Jack said nothing.

"That mother of hers is only half there," Mrs Fosdyke went on. "Less than half. There's no wonder that child's out of control."

Still Jack waited. This was not his cue.

"It'll be months before that room's set to rights," continued Mrs Fosdyke. "Months and months. And I suppose you'll all be eating in the kitchen under my feet till then. Yes. Well, that'll be nice, I must say. Very nice."

Jack began to wonder whether Mrs Fosdyke talked like this all the time, whether there was anyone else there or not, asking herself questions and answering them and changing from one subject to another. He began to suspect that his cue never would come up. Another thing was that she was always moving round and half the time he had his back to her. He did not feel that he could create a Mysterious Impression with his back. He got up, and stood waiting around for her to say something else.

"There's butter gone up again two pence a pound." Mrs Fosdyke was off on a new tack. She turned from the sink and Jack stepped into her path so that she would have to look at him and notice something faraway about him, but all she did was scoot round him and next minute had her back to him, shaking dusters out of a drawer.

"Mrs Bagthorpe," soliloquised Mrs Fosdyke, "says there is more actual vitamings in marge than there is in butter. But that's no comfort, the price marge is."

Jack was just wondering whether he ought to make a few low moaning noises or something when the telephone rang and Mrs Fosdyke scuttled out to answer it.

"Oh, my good gracious!" he heard her say, followed by a series of disbelieving cries on an ascending scale. Then the telephone was put down.

"Mr Parker!" she poked her head in. "House gone up in flames – oh, would you – oh, I'd best go and tell them!"

She was down again in two minutes and started putting the kettle on and rattling cups and saucers.

"You can't hardly believe it," she said. "I thought I should've dropped dead when he told me. Sounded cool as a cucumber, mind. 'Just let 'em know I've got my own little blaze going,' he says, or something like that."

On she rambled. Jack was by now thoroughly fed up with Mrs Fosdyke. She had refused to look at him and notice that he was doing a Mysterious Impression, and now she was telling Jack a piece of news he already knew – had known over an hour ago. There are few more frustrating things in life than being told something that you already know but cannot admit to knowing.

He decided to go up to his room and practise doing his Mysterious Impression in front of a mirror.

"Come on, Zero."

He did not want Zero to be lying there looking so comfortable when Mr Bagthorpe came down, because he would probably get irritated by this and start in on Zero again and undo all the good work Jack had been doing on him. As Jack went out he heard Mrs Fosdyke telling herself:

"If I could remember for the life of me whether I turned my gas off under those prunes, I'd feel better. Things always go in threes. There'll be a third."

The way Jack felt at that moment about Mrs Fosdyke he rather hoped her prunes would set fire to her house – in a minor way, anyhow.

He met his mother on the landing. Her Yoga did not seem to have worked very well this morning, or else the calmness had worn off already.

"I must get over there and see if Celia's all right. Have you heard? Oh, it's dreadful, terrible!"

"It's Daisy again, I expect," Jack said. "It didn't sound all that bad from what Mrs F said."

"But Celia – you know how highly strung she is."

"At least no one can say it's Zero's fault this time," Jack said. "Come on, Zero, good boy."

He went into his room. He sat in front of the mirror and began to practise but soon found it was no good. You couldn't do it in a mirror. The whole point was that you had to look *past* somebody, just by their ear, and if you did that to your reflection you couldn't check up on yourself. It didn't matter how quickly you flicked your eyes sideways, you couldn't catch yourself looking past your own ear. You always ended up looking yourself in the eye. Jack gave up.

He took out his notebook and studied it. There wasn't much in it so far. It didn't look like a Plan of Campaign at all. He remembered Uncle Parker's instruction to guard it with his life. He hid it between his comics, where he knew it would be safe. Everybody else in the house despised him for reading them, and said so. They would not, they said, be caught dead looking at them.

By now there was quite a lot of noise downstairs, so Jack decided to go down and have another try at creating a Mysterious Impression. Twice this morning and twice this afternoon, Uncle Parker had said, and he hadn't done it once yet.

"Stay, Zero."

The longer Zero lay low the better, Jack thought. He found the whole family in the kitchen with Mrs Fosdyke darting among them distributing orange juice and toast. Everyone was talking loudly about fires. Mr Bagthorpe was moodily weighing up the chances of both himself and Uncle Parker getting their insurance money when it turned out Daisy had started both fires. It would look like conspiracy to defraud, he said.

"We got our fire in first, though. We get priority. I'll bang the claim in first thing this morning."

Jack sat down. Nobody took any notice of him, including Mrs Fosdyke, who evidently thought he had breakfasted sufficiently already. Everyone but him got orange juice and toast. He began to feel depressed. He began to wonder whether the whole Campaign was not a mistake, and whether to call it off before it even started. Out of a fog he heard his mother's voice:

"… all right, Jack, dear?"

"What? What's that?"

"I said, are you feeling all right. You look a bit pale and funny."

"Oh – yes, oh, I do feel queer!"

His heart began to race. He had done a Mysterious Impression without even trying! He concentrated hard on looking faraway rather than delighted, and must have done it quite well because Mrs Bagthorpe said something about delayed shock.

"I just – just feel sort of faraway," Jack said. He moved his gaze over his mother's left ear and encountered William's stony eyes. Hastily he moved his gaze again over William's ear, and then met Rosie's interested stare.

"You do look queer," she said.

Then Mrs Fosdyke put her oar in.

"And no wonder," she said deflatingly. "A fry-up like that first thing. *I* should've felt queer, a plateful like that. I did tell him, Mrs Bagthorpe – a grapefruit's what you want. I told him, and get your vitamings."

Jack could have killed her.

"Oh, well, perhaps that's it." Mrs Bagthorpe sounded relieved. "There's enough to worry about – nobody else feels as if they've got delayed shock, do they?"

"I do," said Mr Bagthorpe. "So what are you going to do about it?"

He was ignored. He did not mean it. He was just making dialogue, as he did in his TV scripts, and as nobody else in the family was paid for doing this, they did not see why they should play his game. The remark at least drew attention off Jack, who, despite Mrs Fosdyke's untimely intervention, began to feel that he had established some sort of interest in his condition.

When Mrs Bagthorpe said, "You three help Mrs Fosdyke clear and wash up – Jack, you sit where you are and have a nice hot cup of coffee," he decided to mark up his performance as the first authentic Mysterious Impression of the day.

The second was equally difficult to achieve. Jack had always known that his family was an unusually active one, even overactive, but he had never before realised how difficult it was to pin one of its members down and look him or her in the eye. It is very difficult to look someone in the eye when they are reading Voltaire or trying to contact a radio ham in Puerto Rico or painting a portrait. (Rosie had already begun on a second attempt at a Birthday Portrait of Grandma. Grandma had said she had better, because the way she felt, she didn't think she would see another birthday.)

Mr and Mrs Bagthorpe were going to inspect the damage to The Knoll, and Mrs Fosdyke, as Jack now knew, was a congenital non-receiver of Impressions, Mysterious or otherwise.

He opted in the end for trying Rosie and Grandma because both of them seemed basically bored by the idea of the sitting, and would be more likely to spare a glance for himself.

Grandma had opted for having her Portrait painted with the burnt-out shell of the dining-room as a background. Mrs Bagthorpe had protested that this was morbid and unnatural, but Grandma was adamant.

"It was a Sign," she said. "You can't just toss it aside as if it were a mere bubble in the wind. I think I was *meant* to have my Portrait painted in there. If I were not, it wouldn't have burned down."

The logic of this was at the same time hard to follow and irrefutable, and Mrs Bagthorpe had let it go. There was certainly no time to argue with Grandma today. She and her husband had driven off to The Knoll, the latter fulminating.

"It's all go," he said. "Yesterday a fire, today a fire, and on Monday a funeral."

"A funeral!" shrieked Grandma. "Whose?"

"Daisy's," he replied, "if I've anything to do with it."

The sitting began. Jack sat very quietly to begin with. Grandma, against advice, was sitting on the one remaining dining-chair. It had only just survived, and was very charred up and shaky, so Grandma was sitting gingerly. She definitely looked as if she were sitting on a chair she expected to collapse at any moment. In some ways Jack could see this was a good thing because it gave her a more than usually wide-awake expression.

When Rosie had been sketching for a while he peered over to look. He saw that Rosie was getting plenty of the burnt-out background in. She had liked this idea as well as Grandma, and said it would give the portrait atmosphere and make it stand out. As yet Grandma's face had no features and it still looked like the one that had gone up in flames. It was hard to think of anything to say about the portrait in its present state but Jack thought he had better try in case his silence was misconstrued as disapproval. He did not, however, attempt anything like a critical appraisal.

"Jolly good, Rosie," he said. "I like the way you've got those tattered curtains dangling at the back."

"What about me?" demanded Grandma. "How am I going?"

"Jolly well, Grandma," he assured her. "It's going to be much better than the other one when it's finished."

"It'll be the last, of course," Grandma remarked. "Last night put years on me."

"If you could last a few more years you'd get a better portrait," Rosie said, opening up her paints. "Everyone seems to keep forgetting I'm only eight and expects me to be Augustus John or Leonardo da Vinci or something.

I think if I get my portraits looking even a *bit* like people they ought to be satisfied."

"You're putting my eyes in, I hope," Grandma enquired suspiciously, "and my nose?"

Jack stepped hastily in to save Rosie.

"I have a feeling," he said, quite off the cuff, "a strange feeling, that you will live to be a hundred, Grandma."

"What*ever* is the child saying?" said Grandma. She looked keenly at him and Jack, who was getting to recognise cues when they occurred, allowed his eyes to move slowly past her right ear. There he saw roast beef and Yorkshire pudding swimming in gravy and surrounded by crisp roast potatoes.

"Why," he heard Grandma demand, "do you not look me straight in the eye when I speak to you?"

Jack held his roast beef steady and murmured,

"I see… I see…"

"What are you looking at?" A note of alarm had crept into Grandma's voice. "Is there someone behind me?"

It was at this point that Jack overstepped the mark. If he had kept his head, and simply passed a hand over his eyes and shaken himself and said dreamily, "Oh… oh… that was queer… where am I?" a Mysterious Impression would have been created without any unwelcome side effects. But Grandma's suggestion that there might be somebody behind her gave Jack such scope of expansion that he could not resist it. By means of adding treacle tart and custard to his Vision he deepened his gaze and said again,

"I see… I see…"

Grandma, who was a game old lady, did not wait for him to say what he saw. She turned rapidly in her charred chair to see for herself. The chair broke and Grandma went sideways. Jack and Rosie both leapt to her aid and the paints and easel went over.

Everything was very confused from then on. Tess and Mrs Fosdyke arrived on the scene. (William did not hear the racket because he had his headphones on.) Grandma was lying on the sodden carpet refusing to be helped up.

"I shall stay here until I am able to get up by myself," Grandma kept saying, while Rosie was sobbing over her ruined Portrait. She accused Jack of having staged the whole thing on purpose to pay her back for beating him at swimming. This he hotly denied and a first-class row developed during which he told Rosie what he had really thought of her Portrait anyway.

"First portrait *I've* ever seen without eyes… and nose," he said. "Since yesterday, anyway."

At this Grandma, who had half raised herself up, sank back again.

"No eyes," she cried despairingly. "No nose, no mouth. How could you, Rosie?"

"I hadn't finished!" Poor Rosie redoubled her sobs. "It would've been lovely – I *was* going to have done eyes and things."

Grandma was not really listening.

"I think I know a Sign when I see one," she was saying, to herself, mainly. "There can have been few people in history who have had their Birthday Cake go up in flames and their Birthday Portraits ruined in less than a day. Even Job had his troubles spaced out. If ever I do manage to move from here, I shall probably go to bed and stay there."

"Oh, come along, Grandma, do. Let me help you," pleaded Tess. "I've got a Judo Club meeting in half an hour, and I can't go and leave you there. I'm the oldest while William has his headphones on."

"Two Portraits in twenty-four hours," Grandma went on. "Eyeless Portraits. Noseless. Mouthless. It's horrible."

At this Rosie flung her ruined Portrait down, stamped on it, and ran from the room. Then Mr and Mrs Bagthorpe returned, the former in an even worse mood than when he had left. He and Uncle Parker had had a few savage exchanges and parted, which was why the visit had been so brief. Finding Grandma on the floor did not improve his temper. At first he thought she was lying down there because this was how she wanted to pose.

"I suppose you think you look like Ophelia?" he enquired sarcastically. "Or a reclining Muse?"

At this point Jack slunk off to join Zero. He had a definite feeling that whatever was later remembered of this whole episode, it would not be his own Mysterious Impression.

Chapter Five

Jack was in a dilemma. Not only was he having trouble with a build-up of Mysteriousness to his final Vision of the Lavender Man Bearing Tidings, but now he was no longer certain that the Lavender Man would be coming anyway, with or without Tidings. If Jack said a Lavender Man was coming and he turned up, that was one thing, but if he did not, that would be another again.

They'd probably have me put away, he thought. *They're ashamed of me enough as it is. I'm just an embarrassment to them, not being a genius.*

The way Mr Bagthorpe was currently talking it did not sound as if Uncle Parker would be crossing his threshold again for a long time to come. He actually said as much. On the other hand, Mr Bagthorpe and Uncle Parker had so many rows that one suspected that they rather enjoyed them, and Jack himself had certainly noticed some of their interchanges turning up later pretty well word for word in Mr Bagthorpe's television scripts. Indeed, so had Uncle Parker himself (though he usually affected to be too busy to watch Mr Bagthorpe's programmes, or any television at all, for that matter). He said loudly and often that he regarded it as a debased and debasing medium. But during one of their rows Uncle Parker had threatened that he would sue Mr Bagthorpe unless he paid him a fair percentage for the dialogue he had unwittingly supplied, as anything that he, Uncle Parker, might say was copyright.

There was no way of finding out what was happening at The Knoll because if Jack himself went there then the Bagthorpes would immediately put two and two together when the Lavender Man appeared, and the whole game would be up before it got properly started. The one chance Jack did have was to make a telephone call. Even this was fraught with danger. The two telephones in the house were sited in the hall and in Mr Bagthorpe's study. The hall was little better than a public thoroughfare, and too close to Mrs Fosdyke's HQ in the kitchen, and of course Mr Bagthorpe was there in the study along with his telephone, probably making notes on his recent interchange with Uncle Parker.

I'll go down into the village and use the phone box there, Jack thought. *Then, if Aunt Celia answers I can put the phone straight down and keep trying till I do get Uncle Parker. No one'll know who it is if I don't speak.*

After lunch, which was a tense, relatively silent affair with Grandma, Grandpa and Rosie all missing, Jack set off to the village with Zero. The walk gave Jack another chance to give Zero a pep talk, because he could not hope to keep out of Mr Bagthorpe's way for ever and needed building up as much as possible before the inevitable meeting took place.

"Don't forget," Jack told Zero, "that half the things he says he doesn't mean. He only says things to try out how they sound, in case he can use them in his scripts. Remember that."

Zero's legs had now stopped shaking and he was obviously making progress. He had had the ordinary kind of shock rather than the delayed variety Mrs Bagthorpe had been talking about.

When he reached the village Jack took a quick look about to see if anybody who knew him was looking. Then he went into the booth and took Zero in as well, even though it did make things rather crowded about his feet.

Jack stood with his back to the road and dialled Uncle Parker's number. It rang for some time before the receiver was lifted and a voice, high and clear and unmistakably Daisy's, said:

"Hello, Thurton four-oh-one Daisy Parker speaking. I nearly burnded the house down today and yesterday as well. Do you want Mummy or Daddy?"

Jack hastily replaced the receiver. He waited a minute or two to let Daisy get clear of the phone, then dialled again. Again Daisy's voice replied:

"Hello. Thurton four-oh-one. Daisy Parker speaking. Is it whoever jus' rung? If not, I nearly burnded the house down today and yesterday as well. If so will you please hang on this time and don't go away like you did last."

Jack replaced the receiver. This time he left the booth and walked on, trying to think of a way round what looked like an impasse. The game with Daisy could go on all afternoon, he could see that. His money would run out.

What could I do to scare her off? he wondered. *What's she scared of?*

There was not, in fact, very much that Daisy was scared of. She was not half so scared of things as four-year-olds are supposed to be. He had actually heard Uncle Parker telling Mrs Bagthorpe this. It was unnatural, he said. He had given up reading her Red Riding Hood and Jack and the Beanstalk and so on because when he got to the bits about wolves and giants and such, she just laughed. It was no fun, he said, reading scary tales to four-year-olds that just laughed. It made you look a fool. The only thing she was scared of, apparently, was Daleks and deathrays and things, and he was most certainly not having any of that rubbish in his house. He would not, he declared, be caught dead reading about Daleks and deathrays.

Jack pondered a few minutes perfecting his scheme and retraced his steps to the kiosk. Sure enough, it was Daisy's voice he heard.

"That is Daisy Parker," said Jack, interrupting her. He used a disguised voice. His acting had improved considerably in the course of the day, and the voice came out quite well. "You will be exterminated."

He heard a squeal at the other end of the line.

"We shall transmit a deathray through the telephone wire," said Jack. "You are holding the telephone, and it will exterminate you!"

There was a really loud shriek then, followed by a clatter that nearly deafened Jack. The receiver had not been replaced, he realised, but let drop on to the stone floor of the hall. In the background he could hear Daisy squealing and then Aunt Celia's voice and very faintly, Jack was certain, Uncle Parker's own. He hung on in case it was he who came to the phone, but in the end it was Aunt Celia's footsteps he heard approaching, and her voice that said:

"Hellooooo, Helloooo. Is anyone there?"

Jack, elated by his dramatic success with Daisy, was tempted to threaten her with extermination too, but resisted.

"In any case," he told himself as he replaced the receiver, "she'd probably have hysterics or something and Uncle Parker'd murder me when he found out."

Uncle Parker, for some obscure reason, loved Aunt Celia to distraction. He seemed to have a blind spot about her.

Jack took Zero for another short walk and returned yet again to the kiosk.

"Keep your fingers crossed," he told Zero, and dialled.

"Hallooo, hallooooo... Celia Parker here..."

Jack banged the telephone down. At intervals of five or ten minutes he dialled four times more. On the last two occasions Aunt Celia was not answering very calmly. She was saying things like:

"Who are you – leave me alone, leave me alone!" and:

"I know there's someone there – I can hear you breathing... Who are you, who? Are you human?"

"One more time," he told Zero. His supply of money had almost run out. He waited a whole quarter of an hour before making the final call. This time, Uncle Parker's voice answered. There were no preliminaries.

"Look," said Uncle Parker's voice, "I don't know who you are, but you are a maniac and a public nuisance. You have reduced my wife and only child to hysteria."

"It's me!" shouted Jack, lightheaded with relief. "It's me – Jack!"

"There is a law about this sort of thing," went on Uncle Parker, astoundingly, "and innocent subscribers must be protected from fiends like yourself. One more call from you, and I shall call the police."

Jack wondered whether he had gone mad.

"Look, all I want to know is, are you still coming in that lavender suit, or not?"

"And when I say I am going to do a thing," said Uncle Parker, "I do it. Understand?"

The line went dead. Slowly Jack replaced his own receiver.

Of course, he thought, *Aunt Celia was listening. He had to pretend it was... And what was it he said at the end – 'When I say I'm going to do a thing, I do it.' That was it – that was his way of giving me the answer.*

He pushed open the door and went out.

"Come on, Zero!"

He was going to try to pull in one more Mysterious

Impression before coming out with the actual Vision One at tea-time. He found himself excited and pleased by the prospect. Things had become so lively during the past twenty-four hours that he was beginning to enjoy it, and feel let down when they slackened off.

On his way across the fields he had the good fortune to pick up a couple of twigs that looked promising from the dowsing point of view. He even tried holding one out for some distance, but nothing happened.

It's because I don't know the proper grip, he thought. *It's how you hold it that counts*.

He hid the twigs in his wardrobe when he got home and then went down to survey the field. Grandpa had surfaced, he noticed, but was still without his hearing aid. He was nodding over a copy of *The Guardian*. Mrs Fosdyke was banging about in the kitchen baking.

"Where's Mother?" he asked.

"Doing her Problems," Mrs Fosdyke replied briefly. "And don't want disturbing, I don't suppose. You'd think she had enough problems of her own."

Mrs Bagthorpe had an Agony Column in a monthly journal under the name of Stella Bright. She got hundreds of letters every week, and some of them, she said, were really agonising. This was partly why she had taken up Yoga, to help restore her balance. She was also a magistrate in a juvenile court and so she saw a lot of the hard side of life. Mr Bagthorpe was always trying to pump her about her letters and her cases, to see if he could get some good material for his scripts, but she refused to be drawn.

"A veil of secrecy must be preserved," she always said. (This was where William had got it from.) "These are sacred confidences. I am morally bound by a Confessional Oath."

She kept all her letters locked in a cupboard because she did not altogether trust Mr Bagthorpe not to go rummaging about if he ever got really desperate for an idea. Every few weeks there was a ritual called The Agony Bonfire. The closed files of letters would be brought out and ceremonially burnt. Mrs Bagthorpe always supervised this herself, especially if there were a high wind when she would get nervous in case a particularly agonising letter got blown out of the garden and fell into the wrong hands. She would not leave the bonfire until it had died right down and even then would prod about among the ashes with a hoe to make sure there were no charred remains (particularly if Mr Bagthorpe was hovering about at the time). She was exceedingly thorough about her Problems, and took them very seriously.

Once or twice Mr Bagthorpe, during periods when he was stuck with his scripts and at a loose end, had written some bogus letters to Stella Bright with false names and using the addresses of a film producer friend in Islington and one in Fulham. They had been real stingers, he afterwards gleefully informed the rest of the family, though he would not divulge most of the details, saying that they were too young for that sort of thing. Mrs Bagthorpe had fallen straight into the trap and written back as requested in the stamped addressed envelopes provided. Sometimes when he and his wife had a row Mr Bagthorpe would sardonically refer to this and quote extracts from Stella Bright's replies, punctuated by scornful laughs. He had even gone so far as to write a TV script about the incident but the BBC had turned it down. He was not downcast by this and would boast that his script had been "too hot to handle". It was easy to see why Mrs Bagthorpe did not trust him and kept all her letters locked up.

If his mother was up in her room doing her column Jack knew she would not be favourably inclined to receive a Mysterious Impression. Mrs Fosdyke was automatically disqualified and Grandpa by now had his head right down and looked dead to the world. The whole house was depressingly quiet, and nobody would at that moment have taken it as the haunt of genius.

Jack wandered out into the garden with Zero following. He came upon Mr Bagthorpe so suddenly that it was too late to dodge out of sight. What Mr Bagthorpe was doing was trying to plant a pot-grown tree some fifteen feet high, single-handed. He was trying to hold it upright and fill in the hole at the same time, without much success.

"Come and hold this," he ordered on catching sight of Jack, who obediently went and held the tree while Mr Bagthorpe seized his spade and began to shovel his specially mixed soil in round it. Zero must have missed Mr Bagthorpe's scent, being out of doors, and was probably still in a mild state of shock, because he wandered over and sniffed at the soil.

"Doesn't it irritate the hell out of you having that hound trailing you round everywhere?" said Mr Bagthorpe. "It would me. It'd drive me to drink."

"He likes me," said Jack. "It's a compliment. And I like him," he added boldly, knowing that Zero was listening and would soon become undermined if no one stood up for him.

"You must be joking," said Mr Bagthorpe.

"We've got a lot in common," Jack said sturdily.

"Really? You got pudding feet and no brains and matted fur, have you?"

Jack was so annoyed by this that he refused to answer. He even had a sudden crazy idea that he might report Mr Bagthorpe to the RSPCA if he could get some tapes of him criticising Zero. It could be classed as mental cruelty.

"Is it up straight?" asked Mr Bagthorpe, deeply involved in his hole. Jack refused to answer this too. In point of fact the tree was not particularly straight, because it was too tall for Jack to handle and Mr Bagthorpe was treading it in all lopsided. But it seemed to Jack that if his father's tree got put in at an angle, however acute, it would be no more than justice. Nobody could expect to insult people and get them to hold trees straight as well.

Mr Bagthorpe threw down his spade and stepped back. He surveyed Jack and the tree.

"I suppose I should've had more sense than ask you," he said finally.

At this point, Jack scented the cue for a Third Mysterious Impression. He fixed his eyes, quite deliberately, just past his father's left ear.

"What're you looking at?" demanded Mr Bagthorpe and whirled about, scanning the garden. Jack was looking at a plateful of the jam tarts and scones Mrs Fosdyke was baking.

"Look at me," commanded Mr Bagthorpe. Jack pretended not to hear and held his gaze steady. This, surprisingly, unnerved Mr Bagthorpe quite quickly.

"What's going on?" he said uneasily, and had another

thorough scan round. Then, "I don't get it. Here, give me that tree."

Jack released his grip on the tree and it swooped down on to Mr Bagthorpe.

"Get out of here!" Mr Bagthorpe's face glowered through a latticework of branches and leaves. "And take that hound of hell with you."

Jack turned silently and walked off.

"It's that mutton-brained hound that's at the bottom of this!" he heard Mr Bagthorpe yelling after him. Jack broke into a run and did not stop till he was out of earshot, mainly for Zero's sake.

"Good boy!" He stopped and patted him hard. "Don't you take any notice. He's just jealous."

Zero wagged his tail feebly.

Jack had not intended to count this as a successful Mysterious Impression till half an hour later he heard his mother and father talking in the burnt-out dining-room. They were in there deciding on a new colour scheme.

"… suffering from delayed shock, this morning," he heard Mrs Bagthorpe say.

"If that was delayed shock, I'm the Emperor of Siam," came Mr Bagthorpe's terse reply. "I tell you he was looking past my left ear like he was Joan of Arc seeing visions, or something."

Jack, listening, glowed and expanded and awarded himself an Oscar.

"Perhaps he was hallucinating." Mrs Bagthorpe sounded genuinely concerned and Jack felt half guilty. "That can be a symptom of delayed shock."

"Oh, do be quiet about delayed shock," Mr Bagthorpe told her. "You've got it on the brain. It's clear as crystal what's happening. That boy's mooning round from morning till night with no one for company but that half-witted mongrel of his, and he's beginning to get like him. It's a perfectly well-recognised and authenticated phenomenon. You've heard about people growing like their dogs, for heaven's sake?"

"Don't be silly," returned his wife. "It's quite ridiculous the way you go on about that dog. As a matter of fact, I rather like him."

Jack did not wait to hear what followed. Mr Bagthorpe was still spluttering and Jack could not wait to get back to his room and tell Zero, in all honesty, that Mrs Bagthorpe liked him as well.

"D'you hear? She *likes* you. Good old Zero."

Zero thumped his tail once or twice and Jack was delighted, and thought:

So now, there's only the actual Vision to go.

To put things on a businesslike footing he took out his

loose-leaf notebook and wrote "Mission Accomplished" after "Create Mysterious Impressions". He then listed them as:

1. By accident at breakfast but thought to be delayed shock.
2. On Grandma while Rosie was doing her portrait which unfortunately got spoiled.
3. On Father I'm glad to say while he was planting his rotten lopsided tree.

He put the book back among the pile of comics and spent the rest of the time till tea rereading some back numbers.

Everyone had gathered in the kitchen for tea in a state of what seemed uneasy truce. Jack guessed that what had brought them all together was not so much the desire for a brisk and lively interchange of ideas as the delicious scent of Mrs Fosdyke's cooking, which had been invading the house and garden all afternoon. (Even Mr Bagthorpe conceded that Mrs Fosdyke did not *cook* like a hedgehog.) Three people present had also missed lunch, of course. Rosie was evidently still blaming Jack for the ruination of her second Birthday Portrait and pulled truly horrible faces whenever he looked at her. These he did not return, partly because he felt he was too old to be caught doing this, and partly because he recognised that he had, albeit in a roundabout and quite unintentional way, brought about the catastrophe. He resolved that on some future occasion he would make it up to her, either by buying her an ice lolly or letting her borrow his microscope, which as a rule he would lend to no one, even when bribed.

Conversation to begin with was sporadic and Jack decided to wait until it warmed up before coming out with his Lavender Man Bearing Tidings. Had he known, of course, that things were to warm up to the point where nobody would be able to hear a word anybody else was saying, his strategy might have been different.

It started innocently enough with Tess announcing as she reached for her third buttered scone that she might give up Judo and take up Yoga instead.

"Bit tactless, isn't it?" enquired Mr Bagthorpe tactlessly.

"Why is it?"

"I should hardly have thought," he replied, "that it needed to be spelled out. I should have thought you might have left the monopoly of Yoga to your mother."

"I don't see why," Tess said. "I don't see why we can't both do it."

"All right, I'll *spell* it out," said Mr Bagthorpe, "if that's the way you want it. The way your mother does her Yoga, she looks like someone doing an impression of a dinosaur emerging from the primeval mud."

There was a silence.

"Someone will have to come with me to have it fitted," said Grandpa suddenly, obviously finishing a train of thought he had started in his head.

"If you took any form of physical exercise yourself," said Mrs Bagthorpe distantly, "you would be in a position to make that kind of criticism. Though even then there are those who would think it not only uncalled-for, but unkind."

"I've never seen you doing your Plough Posture and things," said William, "but you certainly don't look like a dinosaur most of the time."

"Thank you, William," said his mother, accepting this dubiously worded testimony.

"I bet you can't stand on your head anyway, Father," piped up Rosie.

"No use at all," said Grandpa loudly. "Worse than useless."

"Rubbish," snapped Mr Bagthorpe. "Just wait while I swallow this mouthful."

He got up from the table.

"What are you going to do?" cried Mrs Bagthorpe. "You're not going to stand on your head now, in the middle of a meal?"

"And make sure he sees me do it," Mr Bagthorpe indicated Grandpa.

"But he was talking about hearing aids," began his

wife, but too late. Mr Bagthorpe was already crouched in preparation.

"Stop him, Mother," she implored.

"Henry has always gone his own way," said Grandma imperturbably. She was, after all, Mr Bagthorpe's mother, and should know. "And he has always been a show-off."

Mr Bagthorpe was halfway up when he heard his own mother so slander him. Everyone watched fascinated as he swayed up there, uncertain whether to carry on and complete the headstand, or to surface and answer back. Gravity decided the matter. Mr Bagthorpe could not, unless he had been doing it secretly in his study, have stood on his head since he was a schoolboy, and it showed. His descent was not graceful. He crashed down and as his legs skewered round one of his shoes caught a Dresden piece on the dresser. A chair also went over. Everyone present, except Grandpa and William, shrieked. (Grandpa was still making loud observations about hearing aids and William was helpless with laughter.) Mrs Fosdyke shrieked louder than anyone and darted vainly forward to try to field the Dresden piece before it hit the tiles. The crash took place under her very nose.

"Oh no! No! Not me Dresden," she lamented. It was this kind of scene that made her persistently refuse to live in at the Bagthorpes'. The reason she always gave for this was that she had her unmarried son to cook for. The real reason, as she told her friends, was that certainly Mr Bagthorpe and Grandma, and possibly more of the family, were mad, and that the continual goings-on would be more than flesh and blood could stand. She felt it would shorten her life.

She later gave a graphic picture of Mr Bagthorpe's Yogic exhibition to her cronies in The Fiddler's Arms.

"With a brain like his," she opined, "you can't afford to have the blood rushing to your head. It unhinged him, of course, and down he comes, crash on my Dresden Floral, and that's that. Broke his arm as well, and I wish no harm to anyone, I'm sure, but it served him right."

The confusion that followed Mr Bagthorpe's collapse was certainly exceeding. Jack actually bawled above the din:

"I see a Lavender Man Bearing Tidings," but he might as well have been reciting the two times table. Everybody else was bawling too.

Grandma was wailing, "Son, son, speak, speak!" like someone out of the Old Testament.

Rosie jumped up and down yelling, "I knew he couldn't do it, I knew he couldn't do it!" until Tess administered a sharp slap and set her off bawling instead.

Mrs Bagthorpe, with creditable concern, all things considered, rushed forward and pushed Grandma aside.

"Henry, are you hurt?"

"My arm, my arm!" bellowed Mr Bagthorpe above the din. "Ow – OUGH!" as his wife tried to raise him, and then, in tones of epic despair:

"My writing arm! My God, it's my writing arm!"

William was sent to telephone the doctor. Mr Bagthorpe, supporting his right arm with his left, was led into the sitting-room and made comfortable with cushions (or as comfortable as he would admit to being).

Even then the tumult did not abate because in true Bagthorpe tradition a post-mortem inquiry into the incident was instantly set up and everybody started arguing about whose fault it had all been. Jack blamed Mr Bagthorpe himself for starting the whole thing off with his rude remarks about dinosaurs. Tess blamed Rosie for daring him, and William for laughing at him just when he was at his most precarious. Grandma blamed Grandpa for making one of his loud remarks off cue, and it seemed as if it was going to be one of those rare occasions when it was not all finally pinned on to Zero. (Zero had been left upstairs. Jack had given him the job of guarding the pile of comics in which the Plan of Campaign was concealed, in the hope that this would give him a sense of responsibility and increase his self-respect.)

Jack looked at his watch. It was already after five and

time was short. The furore showed no sign of dying down and would doubtless redouble when the doctor arrived and each Bagthorpe made his or her own diagnosis. The only person in the room who could actually be pinned down, Jack decided, was the patient himself, who was at least sitting. He had gone quiet now, except for the occasional groan, because for the time being he had an inattentive audience on which any serious performance would be wasted.

It was hard on him, Jack realised, to have to receive two Mysterious Impressions so close together, particularly on top of injuring his writing arm, but there seemed no choice. He advanced and stood in front of Mr Bagthorpe's chair waiting to be noticed. At last his father's eyes travelled up and met his.

"What're you hanging about there for?" demanded Mr Bagthorpe. "Where's that doctor got to? This could be the end of the road for me. I'm sunk without my right arm."

Jack really had to harden himself to carry through the manoeuvre. Slowly he moved his gaze to just behind Mr Bagthorpe's right ear, and visualised turkey with all the trimmings, which he obviously would not get in the foreseeable future, but there was no harm in imagining. The effect was gratifyingly dramatic.

"Quick! Help! He's doing it again!" yelled Mr Bagthorpe.

He yelled so loud he even got heard and everyone looked round.

"Quick! Laura – look! It's horrible! I told you – look – he's doing it again!"

Mrs Bagthorpe rushed over and the others, interested, crowded round.

"Get behind me, Laura, quick!" commanded Mr Bagthorpe, "and just look where he's got his eyes fixed."

Jack did not feel he could sustain his performance much longer. He had only begun his acting career that morning, and the size of the present audience was daunting. Just as Mrs Bagthorpe crouched behind her husband's chair to take a bearing on the line of Jack's gaze, he said, quite distinctly and slowly, "I see a Lavender Man Bearing Tidings."

The hush that now fell was total.

"He sees what?" hissed Grandma at last, poking Tess. "What's that about lavender bags?"

"He says he sees a Lavender Man Bearing Tidings, Grandma," Tess whispered back.

"Oh."

Jack repeated the words. He then stepped back and passed a hand over his eyes and murmured, "Where am I?" once or twice, just to round the whole thing off.

It was Mr Bagthorpe who broke the silence.

"When that doctor does come," he said, "get him seen to first. My own can wait. Poor old chap. Completely bananas. He'll end up in a straitjacket."

"Someone'll have to come with me to get it fitted," said Grandpa loudly in the ensuing silence.

Chapter Six

When the doctor eventually arrived Mr Bagthorpe insisted that he examine Jack immediately.

"Don't worry about me," he said faintly, leaning back on his cushions, "I shall survive. I think my writing arm may be a write-off – ha, that's good!" (He perked up momentarily but sank back again.) "But that boy must be examined."

"What for?" asked Dr Winters. He looked keenly at Jack, who had been trying so hard to appear normal during the last half-hour that the strain was beginning to tell. When the family cross-examined him about the Lavender Man Bearing Tidings while waiting for the doctor, he stoutly denied all knowledge of saying any such thing, and said they must all have been dreaming.

"I just felt a bit giddy, that's all," he told them. "Like I did earlier. Everyone gets it sometimes."

"I don't," William said.

The rest of them promptly chimed in, saying they never got giddy either, with the exception of Grandma who said that she got giddy so often nowadays that she could hardly tell the difference.

"Who gets giddy and who doesn't has nothing to do with it," Mr Bagthorpe said. "I take it none of us has seen Lavender Men Bearing Tidings?"

They all shook their heads and William said he wouldn't know one if he saw one and was told to shut up.

"This is not a laughing matter," said Mr Bagthorpe sternly. "That boy may not be a genius, but he has always passed as normal – till now."

Jack was so infuriated by this that he very nearly told them he was a lot cleverer than they thought, as witness the fact that the whole tribe of them had been taken in by the first bit of serious acting he had ever done. He managed to refrain from this by promising himself an even greater victory if he stayed his hand.

"I keep telling you," he said, "I'm right as rain. Anyone want to test me on my tables or irregular French verbs?"

Mrs Bagthorpe, who was trying to treat the whole matter

impartially, as she would one of her Problems, thought this a good idea.

"It will at least show whether it's only one part of his brain that has been affected, or all of it," she said sensibly.

So Rosie ran Jack through some mental arithmetic and Tess took him through his French irregular verbs, and he emerged with practically full marks. If anything, he did rather better than could be normally expected. Mr Bagthorpe refused to be comforted by this.

"I don't see that proves anything," he said. "There are plenty of lunatics walking around reeling off kings and queens of England or the Cup Final results for the last twenty years. I know some of them."

"What *do* I have to do to prove I'm normal, then?" Jack asked. He got a dig of his own in. "Stand on my head?"

"Very funny," said Mr Bagthorpe through his teeth.

"As a matter of fact," Tess said, "that was an exceedingly good sign, Jack saying that. A sense of humour is usually regarded as a sign of mental health – apart from excessive punning, which is another matter entirely. That –" she shot a look at her father, who was always doing it – "is often an early indication of impending schizophrenia."

"Thank you very much, Professor Bagthorpe," said William jealously. He had as many Strings to his Bow as Tess had, but knew far fewer long words.

There was every indication that more trouble was brewing when Dr Winters arrived and Mr Bagthorpe put in his urgent request that Jack be immediately examined. Dr Winters did not seem to understand.

"Now what exactly are the symptoms?" he asked.

"He looks all loopy and blank," said Rosie. "I saw him at breakfast."

"I think he has delayed shock, Doctor," put in Mrs Bagthorpe firmly, and Jack gave her a grateful look.

"I'll explain, if you don't mind," Mr Bagthorpe said. "After all, I've seen it twice and nobody else round here has."

"Seen –?" prompted Dr Winters.

"I'll demonstrate." Mr Bagthorpe cleared his throat and stared rivetingly past Dr Winters' head. The latter, bewildered, turned to look behind him.

"I don't see anything," he said.

"Of course you don't!" Mr Bagthorpe told him sharply, annoyed by the failure of his experiment. "There *is* nothing there—" He stopped just short of saying "you idiot" as he would have done had it been a member of the family.

"Ah." The doctor sounded relieved.

"What he does," Mr Bagthorpe told him, "is stare as if he can see Frankenstein or a swarm of angels or something over your shoulder."

Dr Winters addressed himself to Jack directly now.

"You do not, I take it, see either of these things?" he asked.

"No, Doctor," replied Jack truthfully.

"He sees," said Mr Bagthorpe, "which is a good deal worse, I think, a Lavender Man Bearing Tidings."

"A Lavender Man Bearing Tidings?" said the doctor with irritating calmness. "Let's have a look then, shall we?"

The doctor opened his bag and the Bagthorpes watched respectfully while Dr Winters went through the whole performance of looking into Jack's ears, throat and eyes, with particular emphasis on the latter. He also took his temperature and pulse. He then turned and faced his audience.

"There is nothing I can discover," he said carefully, "that would indicate any kind of departure from normal."

"Thank heavens!" Mrs Bagthorpe stepped forward and embraced Jack.

"There *what*?" exploded her disbelieving husband. "You mean to tell me—"

"It was your arm we were called out to examine, I believe," interrupted Dr Winters, preparing to mount his own high horse. "Shall we take a look at this arm?"

Mr Bagthorpe, realising that his whole scriptwriting career might hang upon Dr Winters' goodwill, gave up.

"All right," he said meekly.

"How did it happen?" enquired the doctor.

"I fell over at tea-time," replied Mr Bagthorpe.

This explanation had already been mutually agreed upon by the Bagthorpes. They had decided that so phrased it was the truth without being the whole truth. The Bagthorpes always stuck together at times like this. News of Mr Bagthorpe's disastrous gymnastics would never reach the outside world from Bagthorpe lips. Mrs Fosdyke was another matter. They had long ago given up trying to train her in loyalty.

Dr Winters did not query this explanation. He duly examined the arm and pronounced that it needed to be taken to the nearest hospital, at Aysham, to be X-rayed.

"Tell me the worst," demanded Mr Bagthorpe. "Is it all over?"

"Is what all over?" asked the confused Dr Winters.

"With my career."

With unaccustomed patience Mr Bagthorpe explained that his livelihood, his *raison d'être*, his whole existence depended on the efficient functioning of his right hand, which in turn, he pointed out, depended upon his right arm.

"Most unlikely," Dr Winters snapped his bag shut. "Might be in plaster for a few weeks, that's all."

"In plaster? For weeks?" Mr Bagthorpe fell back again. "It will kill me," he declared.

"Nonsense," said Dr Winters. "Do you good. Give you a chance to catch up on your reading."

"You're not exactly Milton, you know, Father," Tess said unwisely. "It's no good pretending your scriptwriting is 'that one talent it is death to hide'."

"If I am not Milton," returned Mr Bagthorpe, "nor is he me, and can't be expected to know how I feel. If Milton were living at this hour, *he* would be writing TV scripts, let me tell you. And Dickens. And Shakespeare. And Tolstoy. Go and practise your oboe."

Tess stayed where she was.

"Perhaps you could try writing with your toes?" suggested William.

"And type with them as well, I suppose?" said Mr Bagthorpe.

"Now then." The doctor made an effort to terminate his visit. "Are you going to drive your husband to the hospital, Mrs Bagthorpe, or do you want me to arrange transport?"

At that moment there was a violent scream of brakes and a churning of the gravel under the window that could only mean the arrival of Uncle Parker. Jack's heart began to race. None of the others took much notice.

"I can take him, of course," Mrs Bagthorpe was saying, "though it will mean my missing the Parish Council meeting."

"Which is of infinitely greater consequence than my entire writing career, of course," said Mr Bagthorpe, who had evidently decided to stop being brave and make an all-out bid for sympathy instead.

At that moment in breezed Uncle Parker.

"Hello, all!"

The Bagthorpes turned. There was silence. Uncle Parker was attired in an elegant suit, complete with waistcoat, of palest lavender. He wore a purple bow tie and black patent shoes.

"News," he announced, "I've got news!"

The Bagthorpes boggled. Then, one by one, they swivelled their gaze to Jack himself, as if they expected to see him in some way changed, transmogrified, now that his prophecy was fulfilled. Jack wondered briefly whether he should do his trance performance again, but decided against it. He had, after all, denied all knowledge of having said anything about a Lavender Man Bearing Tidings. In any case, he had done enough acting for one day.

Still the Bagthorpes were transfixed and even Dr Winters was visibly shaken and looking at Jack again, as if for something he had missed in his first examination.

There came into the hush a high, dismal, prolonged howl. The already shocked Bagthorpes now positively froze.

"What… what on earth…?" began Mrs Bagthorpe faintly.

The howl came again.

"It's a werewolf, I think," said Rosie in a small voice and shuffled up to her mother.

"Crikey! It's Zero!"

Jack dashed from the room. Zero, who had been patiently guarding the pile of comics for a full two hours now, evidently needed urgently to leave the house. When Jack opened his bedroom door he was practically knocked sideways as Zero hurled himself forward and shot down the landing.

"Sorry!" yelled Jack after him. He himself leapt down the stairs two at a time and into the sitting-room. He could not afford to miss anything. By now the Bagthorpes, to some extent recovered, were beginning to find their tongues.

"Didn't expect to find you here, Doctor," Uncle Parker was saying. "No one ill, I trust?"

"Only me," said Mr Bagthorpe. "Started any good fires lately?"

"Mr Bagthorpe has injured his arm in a fall," replied

the doctor. "We were just discussing the problem of transport to the hospital for X-rays."

"No problem," said Uncle Parker. "I'll take him."

"At the moment," said Mr Bagthorpe, "I have only what I suppose in the profession is termed a minor injury. I have no wish, thank you, to arrive at the hospital either crippled for life or a case for the coroner."

Uncle Parker was used to this kind of remark about his driving and took it gracefully.

"As you like," he said, "but you've only to say the word. Sorry about the arm. How did it happen?"

"He fell over at tea-time," said several Bagthorpes in unison. Uncle Parker, as one of the family, would hear the truth later, but not now, in the presence of an outsider.

"A Lavender Man Bearing Tidings!" Grandma said dramatically and pointed an accusatory finger at Uncle Parker. "That man, the one who ran poor Thomas over, is the Lavender Man."

The other Bagthorpes slowly nodded their heads. There seemed no escaping this conclusion.

"When did you buy that suit?" demanded Mr Bagthorpe. "And where did you get it? Not round here. You don't see suits like that round here, thank God." (Mr Bagthorpe himself usually wore denim as most of his friends at the

BBC did and made a point of looking down-at-heel and interestingly dishevelled.)

"Last week. The West End. D'you like it?" Uncle Parker pirouetted for their benefit.

"It's super," said Tess. "I wish you'd get one like that, Father."

"It's horrible," said Mr Bagthorpe, "but that's beside the point. The point is, it's lavender."

"Unusual, I thought," agreed Uncle Parker.

"Fortunately," returned Mr Bagthorpe. "And wait a minute – what about the tidings?"

"Tidings?" repeated Uncle Parker. He did it beautifully, Jack thought, just a shade of puzzlement – not too much, not too little.

"The Tidings you're Bearing!" Mr Bagthorpe was beginning to shout again.

"I think perhaps I had better explain, Mr Parker," said Dr Winters. "As a matter of fact, we have all just witnessed a most interesting phenomenon."

"You didn't," said Mr Bagthorpe. "*I* did. Twice. And you said there was nothing wrong with him."

Dr Winters ignored the interruption and explained the matter as he understood it much more clearly and briefly than any of the Bagthorpes could have done. Uncle Parker listened admirably. Jack felt that if whatever he did between

8 and 10 a.m. in his study ever fell through, he could easily take up acting instead.

"By Jove!" he exclaimed. "How fascinating. Well, you're a dark horse, young Jack, and no mistake. So we've got a prophet in our midst, have we?"

"A *prophet*?" repeated William disbelievingly, and a shade jealously. "Anyway, the prophecy or whatever it is hasn't come true. You're not Bearing Tidings."

"Ah, but I am," said Uncle Parker. "It's why I came over. I've heard from the Brents."

"About my Danish girl!"

"About my *au pair*!"

Mrs Bagthorpe and Tess exclaimed simultaneously. They both had reason to be delighted. Tess had decided to make Danish another String to her Bow, and it was not on the syllabus at school. Mrs Bagthorpe wanted someone to live in and help with various things Mrs Fosdyke either wouldn't or couldn't do – driving the car, for one thing.

"All fixed up," nodded Uncle Parker. "She arrives tomorrow. Coming in on the 10.59 at Aysham."

"I cannot understand," said Grandma, "why anyone should wish to call a child Atlanta. I am not altogether happy about this arrangement. I am beginning –" with a sideways look at Jack – "to have my doubts about all kinds of things."

"It'll be marvellous," Tess said. "We'll be able to talk Danish all day long. But—"

"So there's your Bearing Tidings," interrupted Mr Bagthorpe. "Is anyone going to do anything about getting me to hospital?"

"Come along," said his wife, "I shall take you. Tess, dear, will you ring Mr Boland and give him my apologies for this evening? And could you, Russell, possibly stop till I get back, and keep an eye on things?"

"We don't need babysitting, you know," said William.

"I know, dear. It's just that, with one thing and another, I'd be happier, at the moment."

In case I have another trance, thought Jack gleefully. *It's worked. It's all worked.*

Mrs Fosdyke poked her head in.

"I'm off," she said briefly. "I've swep' up my Dresden and put the bits in a cereal bowl. It'll never mend."

She shot Mr Bagthorpe a final baleful look, and was gone.

"I can stay for a while," said Uncle Parker, "but I don't want to leave Celia on her own too long."

"Oh – poor Celia – I never asked, how *is* she?" cried Mrs Bagthorpe. "That fire coming so close after the other – she must be quite unnerved."

"She *was* unnerved," said Uncle Parker. "Now, she's

practically unhinged. In fact –" he addressed Dr Winters – "I was in two minds whether to call you and get something to calm her down."

"Whatever's happened now?" asked Mrs Bagthorpe.

"That child's set fire to her school, I expect," said Mr Bagthorpe.

"Some lunatic," said Uncle Parker, "was making anonymous phone calls the whole afternoon. Someone was ringing up and breathing into the phone and then hanging up."

"How ghastly!" Mrs Bagthorpe clasped her hands. "I get this sort of thing, you know, among my Problems. Some poor creatures are hounded to the brink of suicide."

"Really? Tell us more." You could see that Mr Bagthorpe, bad arm or not, was itching to make notes.

She clapped a hand to her mouth.

"No, I mustn't. I can't tell. I can't say."

"What I can say," Uncle Parker duly said, "is that if ever I catch who it was, blood will be shed."

Jack could not look at Uncle Parker. He felt his face burn.

"When I was walking in the garden earlier I saw a hedgehog," stated Grandpa.

"Lovely, Father!" shouted Mrs Bagthorpe encouragingly.

"It was dead," he went on. "I hate to see a dead animal. Unless it's a wasp."

"I'll never forget the day my darling Thomas was killed," began Grandma, "it was—"

"Come on," said Mr Bagthorpe, and got up. "The rest of you, don't let him –" indicating Uncle Parker – "out of your sight. He'll start another fire if you do. He's hooked on it."

He went off to have his arm X-rayed and Jack went to call Zero back in.

Chapter Seven

After Mr and Mrs Bagthorpe and Dr Winters had left everybody started quarrelling. They did not do so immediately, but after Uncle Parker had referred to Jack as The Prophet for about the fifth time.

"What do you mean, Prophet?" demanded William. "There aren't such things nowadays."

"It was just a fluke, you coming up when you did in that suit," said Tess.

"All right, if you're a prophet," said Rosie, "tell us what the weather will be like on Sunday when I go to Debbie Beach's open-air swimming party."

"What an ignorant lot you are," Uncle Parker told them, saving Jack from the necessity of taking up Rosie's challenge.

"There are more things in heaven and earth, let me tell you, than playing tennis and oboes. Young Jack here is, quite clearly, a highly gifted being. Phenomenally gifted, gifted beyond all ken."

"I don't believe it," said William flatly.

"My own theory," continued Uncle Parker, "is that this latent faculty was triggered off by the shock of yesterday's fire. I have done some reading on the subject, and this is quite often the way it happens. In fact I think I may say that I am proud that my own daughter was in part responsible for this marvellous flowering."

"He's not going to start seeing ghosts, I hope," said Grandma. "Because if he is, I might have to leave here and go and live somewhere else."

"He may well see apparitions," nodded Uncle Parker. "Or he may not. None of us yet know the full extent of his powers. It will be a privilege for us all to be able to watch them as they develop."

Jack felt very odd indeed sitting there and hearing himself discussed like this. It all sounded like somebody else.

"There are no such things as ghosts," Tess said.

"Indeed there are," returned Uncle Parker. "I had an aunt who had visitations almost nightly from a monk who had been buried alive centuries before approximately in the spot where her wardrobe now stood."

At this Grandma said she was off out, and left the room.

"I have always felt," said Uncle Parker thoughtfully, "that young Jack here had a kind of – presence. An indefinable power."

"Well, I haven't," said William. "I suppose there's an explanation. That alien intelligence Anonymous from Grimsby was talking about. Perhaps Jack's been taken over by that."

"Trust you to get your everlasting Anonymous from Grimsby in," said Tess scathingly. "Personally, I'm beginning to wonder if he even exists. I think he's a figment of your overheated imagination."

So the row developed. The only one not involved was Jack himself, who sat quietly stroking Zero. One by one the Bagthorpes went stalking off and banging doors were heard in all parts of the house. An oboe started up and a very loud radio signal bleeping. Only Grandfather, Uncle Parker and Jack were left.

"Better do a test," said Uncle Parker. "Can't be too careful. Test if he's being SD…"

He raised his voice to a pitch just above normal.

"Come on, Grandpa," he said. "Let's go and stick into those stuffed eggs now."

Grandpa, who was watching a TV film with the volume turned right off, did not bat an eyelid.

"Right," said Uncle Parker, all at once businesslike. "What about those phone calls then?"

"It was the only way I could think of," said Jack. "I'm sorry, I really am."

"If ever you do a thing like that again," Uncle Parker told him, "I shall skin you alive. Your Aunt Celia has been lying in a darkened room since your last call. She may not write a poem or throw a pot for another month now. Her whole delicate make-up has been rudely shattered."

"I really am sorry," said Jack again. "I never realised it would have that effect on her."

He was evidently forgiven because all at once Uncle Parker's face brightened and he said, "Hey, how about the Lavender Man, then? How about that?"

"It went a bomb," agreed Jack. "Though I had a bit of trouble earlier on with the Mysterious Impressions. I couldn't seem to pin anyone down. I ended up having to do two on Father."

"Do him good," said Uncle Parker heartlessly. "How did he really do his arm?"

Jack told him.

"It's the blight of this whole family," said Uncle Parker when he heard. "Attention-seeking. Exhibitionism. Present company excepted."

"He'll certainly lose his hair if his arm gets put in plaster," said Jack gloomily. "He'll take it out on us. Especially Zero. Does he look better to you than this morning? I've been setting him tasks, to develop responsibility and self-respect."

Uncle Parker gave Zero a cursory glance.

"Looks all right to me," he said. "But you'll never make a silk purse out of a cow's ear. Now look, I've got the next move planned. Two moves. Got your notebook?"

Jack shook his head.

"I've got it concealed in a foolproof hiding place. Only Zero and I know its whereabouts. Shall I fetch it?"

"Haven't time. Any of that lot could be back at any minute. You're going to have to memorise it, I'm afraid. Now. The first thing we have to do is Consolidate. Get that?"

"Consolidate," repeated Jack.

"Write that in your book when you go up, and underline it. What it means is, you want a few more stares past people's ears in the next day or two. Right?"

"Right," said Jack.

"I should give Grandma a miss," Uncle Parker told him. "She's getting jumpy."

"I think I ought to give Father a miss as well," Jack said. "He can't stand it when I look past his ear. It really seems to affect him."

"You've done a jolly good job," Uncle Parker told him.

"Definitely got 'em sitting up. But that lot's not going to settle for just the Lavender Man and the Mysterious Impressions. They're going to want some hard evidence. Without that, Jack, old lad, you'll be a Nine-Day Wonder, and that'll be it. Relegated."

"So what will I do?"

"I'm coming to that. What we shall now mount is a Two-Pronged Attack. The first thing we shall do, is get you properly genned up on the whole subject. I shall offer to fetch that Atlanta creature from Aysham tomorrow."

"They won't let you," objected Jack instantly.

"Oh yes, they will. Your father's out of action, and Laura's in the middle of her Problems. Right?"

"Right," Jack assented.

"There we are, then. Only too glad to take me up. You'll see. They don't seriously think I'll ever kill anyone, you know."

"I think they do," Jack told him. "And I do as well, sometimes."

"Thank you," said Uncle Parker. "I was going to go on to suggest that you come into Aysham with me to a certain shop. But if you feel you're as good as dead meat the minute you step into my car, we'll forget the whole thing."

"Oh no, no!" Jack assured him hastily. "I like going in your car. More like being on the Big Dipper. You know

– exciting. And as long as you wear your seat belt you're all right," he added.

"So that's the first thing," said Uncle Parker. "You must not, of course, be seen accompanying me. I shall pick you up in the village, and you'll have to take a bus back here."

"Where shall I say I'm going?"

"Say what you like. No. Wait. You could say, Mysteriously, 'I have a strong feeling, an urge, to go to Aysham. I feel as if I am being pulled there by an invisible magnet.' Yes. That's good. Say that. Pulls in another Mysterious Impression at no extra cost."

"All right," Jack said, "though I don't like leaving Zero unprotected for too long. I'll have to be back by lunch."

"You will be. And bring your Campaign Book with you."

"What about the other Prong of the Attack?" Jack asked.

"Ah…" Uncle Parker looked suddenly hugely pleased and mysterious. "I have a Manifestation lined up the size of a house. I have up my sleeve a Manifestation that will bring the whole tribe of them to their knees."

"What?" Jack wanted to know. Uncle Parker's excitement was infectious. But he was shaking his head.

"Later. We've been together too long already. We shall be suspected of hatching. Just write Two-Pronged Attack and leave two pages blank. Write Prong One at the top of one page and Prong Two at the top of the other. Got it?"

Jack nodded.

"And now," said Uncle Parker, "I'd be obliged if you'd go and do something noisy elsewhere. I shall help myself to some of your father's gin and tonic and sit here with your grandfather and see if I can guess what that abysmal piece of television is about. I do not normally watch, as you know. The whole medium is debased and—"

"Father's not here," Jack pointed out. "I know jolly well you watch television. No need to keep up the act with me."

"I may watch the odd programme now and again," conceded Uncle Parker. "But to come in halfway through a film with the sound turned down, and work out who's who and what they're all at, is a mental exercise on a par with chess, bridge or *The Times* crossword. Now, clear off and make a noise somewhere."

"I don't see why."

"Because, dear boy," said Uncle Parker patiently, "you will then be registered as having been somewhere other than in here with me. I am the Lavender Man, remember. Your siblings are not exactly the genii they crack themselves up to be but they can, by and large, add one and one."

"I'll go in the garden," Jack said, "and throw sticks for Zero."

"The very ticket," nodded Uncle Parker.

Jack made as much noise as possible in the garden but everyone else was making so much as well that he was probably wasting his time. Rosie was playing the violin and deliberately hitting a lot of excruciating notes, Tess was playing the oboe and William had moved from his radio on to his drums and was doing some of his best tribal stuff. It was at times like this that Mr Bagthorpe would say that he envied Grandpa.

Whether or not Jack was wasting his time making a noise, he was certainly wasting it throwing sticks for Zero, who was notoriously hopeless at this game. It was, Mr Bagthorpe said, his inability to perform this perfectly simple exercise, that marked him out. All dogs could fetch sticks, he said, they were practically born being able to do it.

Jack had never given up trying to train him, though he made sure he never did it when Mr Bagthorpe was around. This was a golden opportunity.

What happened was that Jack showed Zero the stick and then hurled it as far as he could, yelling, "Fetch! Fetch, Zero!" at the top of his voice. When Zero hung back looking confused, Jack raced for the stick and retrieved it himself, at which Zero would become very excited and bark and dance round wagging his tail. He obviously thought this was what the game consisted of, and got some kind of enjoyment out of it. Try as he might Jack could not think of getting through to Zero the message that it was *he* who was supposed to do the fetching.

After nearly an hour of this, by which time he was exhausted while Zero showed every sign of being able to keep up the game for ever, Jack had a sudden inspiration. It seemed to him that if he got down on all fours he would look more like a dog from Zero's point of view, and Zero might then identify with him and begin to imitate him. Jack took a quick glance at the house to make sure no one was looking, then began the experiment.

"Fetch!" he yelled, and hurled the stick. He then dropped down on all fours and scrambled as fast as he could to get it. Zero was obviously thrown by this manoeuvre and kept dodging all round barking furiously and getting in his way. Jack doggedly went the whole distance and as a final desperate bid had the idea of ducking his head and coming up with the stick in his mouth.

"There!" he said through his clenched teeth. "That's the way to do it. Good boy!"

It was very bad luck that Mr Bagthorpe caught him like this. Zero had been making such a racket at the time that Jack had not heard the car until it ground to a halt. He lifted his head, the stick still between his teeth, and encountered the astounded and horrorstruck gaze of Mr Bagthorpe.

He wrenched open the car door shouting, "For God's sake, Laura, get the doctor! Quick!"

Mrs Bagthorpe, after one disbelieving look, uttered a low moan and disappeared into the house. Mr Bagthorpe advanced hesitatingly one or two paces and Jack was so riveted he did not even let go of the stick immediately.

"Now then," said Mr Bagthorpe, in a carefully controlled voice, "it's all right, Jack. It's only me. Here, boy. You let go of that stick and come here."

Jack was so mesmerised that he actually did as he was told. He let the stick drop from his mouth and began to advance on all fours towards his father. Zero kept pace with him. He had given up barking now. This was the effect Mr Bagthorpe always had on him. Afterwards, Jack could never understand why he had acted the way he did. It would have been easy enough just to drop the stick and stand up. The only explanation he could come up with was that Mr Bagthorpe's stare had put him into a state of light hypnosis.

"Good boy," said Mr Bagthorpe soothingly. Then Jack saw his right arm. It was covered from fingers to elbow with smooth white plaster. It was then that the spell broke. Jack got to his feet and he and his father confronted one another for a few seconds at a distance of about twenty yards. Jack had the feeling that Mr Bagthorpe wished to preserve this distance.

"You just stay where you are," he said, "and calm down for a minute. You'll be all right."

"I *am* all right," Jack told him. "Come on, Zero. Good boy."

Mr Bagthorpe dropped back a couple of paces and was right up against the car.

"Look," said Jack. "I'm all right, I tell you."

"I know, I know," said Mr Bagthorpe. Jack was getting irritated by all this soothing. He preferred Mr Bagthorpe as he usually was. He cast round for the best way to get him back to normal. It did not take long.

"I see they've put your arm in plaster," he said. "That's bad luck. That's really rotten luck."

"Bad luck? Bad *luck*?" Mr Bagthorpe's voice threatened to rise right out of its actual range. "It's diabolical, it's unbelievable. It's the end. I can't stand it. I shall go off my head."

There was a pause.

"And that'll make two of us," he said. He gave Jack another uneasy look. "Now you come in, there's a good boy. Just follow me."

He turned and Jack followed and so did Zero. Mr Bagthorpe opened the door of the sitting-room. He just stood there in the doorway staring at something and Jack caught up and peered past his elbow.

The television was silently showing a commercial for toothpaste. Seated in front of it were Grandpa and Uncle Parker, both fast asleep. The latter had his feet up on another chair and a half-finished gin and tonic stood by his elbow.

"Asleep. Me at hospital, having my arm amputated for all he knew, and he goes to sleep!" It was Uncle Parker he meant, not Grandpa. "The man's an emotional cripple. He hasn't a feeling bone in his body."

He moved swiftly forward and pulled away the chair from Uncle Parker's feet. Uncle Parker instantly shot up and stood staring wildly about him and cried, "Fire! Where?"

"You may well ask," returned Mr Bagthorpe grimly. "This house, containing all my scripts and nearly all my relations, could have gone up about your ears for all you'd have known."

"Oh. There isn't one."

Uncle Parker, relieved, sat down again and took a swig of his gin and tonic.

"Easiest thing in the world to drop off in front of television, of course," he said, with intent to infuriate. He caught sight of Mr Bagthorpe's arm.

"Oh, bad *luck*!" he exclaimed sympathetically.

Mr Bagthorpe was enraged by this.

"If anyone says that again," he gritted, "I'll throttle 'em."

"Difficult," murmured Uncle Parker, "with just the one hand."

"I've sent for him. He's coming right over."

As she spoke Mrs Bagthorpe went straight to Jack and put her hand on his forehead. Jack was touched by this. It was a very brave thing to do, if she really thought he was a raving lunatic.

"He feels very hot," she told the others, as if Jack were not there.

"That's because I've been running round for about an hour," Jack said. "Anyone'd be hot."

"Wait till that doctor comes," said Mr Bagthorpe, "I'll sort him out. He's been in practice long enough to recognise a raving lunatic when he's right under his nose."

"What's happened, then?" enquired Uncle Parker with interest. Then, in slightly awed tones, "Has young Jack had another Vision?"

"Vision my elbow," returned Mr Bagthorpe. "I return from an agonising and traumatic ordeal at the hospital to find my own son crouched on all fours in the middle of the lawn with a stick in his mouth, for God's sake."

"Were you?" Even Uncle Parker seemed surprised.

"I'm all right, I tell you." Jack was beginning to feel cornered. "If you've sent for the doctor, you're wasting your time."

"What I always said would happen has finally happened, of course," said Mr Bagthorpe, throwing himself into a chair. "He has gone round with that pudding-footed, mutton-brained hound till it's finally sent him clear out of his mind. I said it would happen. I said it hundreds of times."

Nobody could deny this.

"If you really want to know," said Jack, not seeing how confessing could make things any worse than they already were, "I was training Zero to fetch a stick!"

"Ha!" Mr Bagthorpe let out a sardonic laugh. "That's rich, that is. If we needed any proof, we've got it now. Anyone who thinks that dopey hound could fetch a stick in a million years *has* to be loony. Fetch a stick? Ha!"

"He was beginning to get the hang of it," said Jack sturdily. "I'm sure he was. It's just that nobody had ever shown him properly what to do before. And that's what I was doing."

"Oh dear." Mrs Bagthorpe sat down suddenly. "I don't know what to think."

"None of us knows what to think," said Mr Bagthorpe. "We're losing our minds. Insanity is infectious, you know. You've heard of the Nuns of Loudon?"

"In that case," said Uncle Parker, rising with easy grace. "I'm off. No offence."

"You and that pyromaniac daughter of yours are probably the source of infection," Mr Bagthorpe told him.

"That Danish girl." Uncle Parker paused by the door. "I've got to go into Aysham tomorrow. Pick her up for you, shall I?"

"We've enough on without shipping corpses back to Denmark, thank you," said Mr Bagthorpe.

"Now, just a moment," said his wife. "Let me think a moment. You can't drive, dear."

"Drive?" he gave a hollow laugh. "Drive? Hold a pen? Pick up—"

"No. And I'm right in the middle of my Problems."

"Who," enquired her husband, "is not?"

"And so," concluded Mrs Bagthorpe, "it really would be a help, if it's no trouble, Russell."

"I told you. Got to go in anyway."

"Thank you. But – you will be careful, won't you?" she pleaded.

"I shall drive," Uncle Parker promised her, "like an angel."

"And probably end up being one," said Mr Bagthorpe. "Correction. There's no way you'll end up in heaven, though your passenger might."

"Oh, do stop it, Henry," said Mrs Bagthorpe. "There's no need at all for that sort of talk. I know you've had a trying day—"

"Trying? *Trying?*"

Grandpa woke up.

"I enjoyed that," he said. "Yes, I did." He got up and switched off the television.

"Off up now. Goodnight, all."

"Ah, good evening, Dr Winters," Uncle Parker was saying in the hall. "Good evening again. Just on my way out. The patient's in there, you'll find."

Dr Winters came in and looked wearily about him.

"Now," he said. "What can I do for you this time?"

Chapter Eight

JACK WAS GLAD of the excuse to escape from the house next morning. It was not a happy place to be. Mr Bagthorpe had had a row with Dr Winters the previous evening and was in bed sulking. Grandpa and Grandma had also opted to miss breakfast, the former because he said that until television started there was nothing to get up for till he got his new hearing aid, the latter because she said she could feel her appetite going, probably for good. Mrs Bagthorpe was up to her ears in her Problems and Mrs Fosdyke was still fulminating about her Dresden.

The atmosphere at breakfast was so heavily loaded that Jack found it hard to get in his piece about being drawn to Aysham by an Invisible Magnet. He was, however, determined to do so. Now that he had embarked on the career of being a Phenomenon and a Prophet he felt he owed it to Uncle Parker, as well as himself, to carry it through. It would help Zero too, because there had to be a certain kudos attached to being the chosen dog of a Prophet.

Jack had risen early, taken his Plan of Campaign from between the comics, and done his homework. First he wrote a brief account of his Third Mysterious Impression of the previous day as follows:

> 3. Stared over Father's ear again and he nearly went wild and made Dr Winters look at me before his arm.
> P.S. Also did an accidental MI by showing Zero how to pick up sticks in his mouth. Father thought I thought I was a dog and sent for the doctor again. There was a terrible row.
> LAVENDER MAN BEARING TIDINGS
> This went really well. Uncle Parker is a really good actor and no one can possibly suspect us of plotting (yet).
> We must be very careful to be seen apart, though.

Jack then set out the next few pages of the book. He wrote CONSOLIDATE at the top of one page, underlined it carefully, then underneath wrote "Create as Many Mysterious

Impressions as humanly possible. P.S. Omit Grandma and if possible Father."

The next two pages he headed PRONG ONE and PRONG TWO, again underlining, and leant back. It was very satisfying to have things on this sort of businesslike footing. It gave a kind of order to something that could very easily be taken for blind chaos. It pulled everything together, somehow.

He replaced the notebook, said, "Guard, boy!" to Zero and went down. It was a relief that Mr Bagthorpe was not at breakfast, but the rest of them seemed tacitly to be ganging up on Jack to try to undermine him. He told himself this was a good sign as people only tend to want to undermine their equals, and at the same time last week they would not have thought it worth their while. They set in on him right from the word go.

"Did you sleep well, dear?" enquired Mrs Bagthorpe. She did not ask this anxiously but in a carefree way intended to assure him that she was not really concerned one way or the other.

"Yes, thanks," said Jack.

"Didn't wake up to see a monk on top of the wardrobe, then?" asked William.

"I think you are mixing me up with Uncle Parker's aunt," replied Jack, keeping his cool.

"I thought we'd agreed there were no such things as ghosts," said Tess edgily. (She had slept with her light left on and not had too good a night. She was not, in fact, altogether sure that she hadn't glimpsed a monk on top of *her* wardrobe.)

"I wish I could've seen you with that stick in your mouth," Rosie said in tones as muffled as if she were in the same position, only in her case, the impediment was toast. "You must've looked really silly. Will you go and do it again so's I can take a photo of you?"

"No," replied Jack simply. All he had to do was refuse to be drawn. He had Uncle Parker's promise of a Manifestation the size of a house, and could afford to keep calm.

"I like to keep records of things," said Rosie.

This was true. It was this magpie instinct that had prompted her to secure the autographs of the firemen. It also probably explained why she liked doing portraits.

"Well, darlings, have you all decided what you're going to do today?" asked Mrs Bagthorpe almost gaily.

"Do my Danish," said Tess promptly. "Just think – at lunch we'll all be talking in Danish."

"You speak for yourself," said William.

"I'm going to do a secret portrait of Grandma," Rosie announced. "I feel really sorry for her, getting both the others spoiled. Especially as it wasn't even her fault. I think I'll be able to do it better without her there because she keeps putting me off and asking about her eyes and nose and things."

"Which were, after all, conspicuously lacking from the first two," said William who, when in a bad mood, was not above being sarcastic at the expense of someone only half his age. As it happened, Rosie had an answer.

"There's a very famous portrait of Virginia Woolf without noses and eyes," she said. "So there. It looks just like her, as well."

"And what about you, Jack?" asked Mrs Bagthorpe. He was well aware that it was his movements she was particularly interested in. He recognised that this was the only chance he was going to get to pull in a Mysterious Impression. He looked at his plate instead of her, and said:

"I feel… I feel an urge to go to Aysham…"

"You what?" choked William through a mouthful of coffee.

"I feel as if I am being drawn there by an Invisible Magnet…"

There was a definite silence. Jack kept looking at his plate as if into a crystal ball.

"Father could be right about him, you know," said William at last.

"Oh dear," said Mrs Bagthorpe, "I wish you wouldn't say things like that, Jack."

"Like what?" He did look up now. "All I said was that I felt like going into Aysham."

"That wasn't quite how you put it, dear," said his mother. "I don't know whether I should let you go."

"I'll catch the twenty past nine bus," Jack said. "I'll have to hurry."

"None of you others would like to go in with him, I suppose?" she asked.

"No," they replied promptly in chorus.

Jack was by the door.

"Mother… I suppose… do you think Zero could lie in your room while you're doing your Problems?"

"He's not ill, is he?"

"No," Jack said, "but he might be, if Father comes down and starts calling him names. He'd lie absolutely doggo. You wouldn't know he was there."

"He'd lie quietly chewing up all your letters, but you wouldn't know he was there," said William, not without a degree of justification. Zero had been known to chew paper. The only time Mr Bagthorpe had ever praised him was once in the early days when he had chewed up a telephone bill and a Final Demand for Income Tax.

"You will let him, won't you, Mother?" pleaded Jack.

At this point Mrs Fosdyke pushed brusquely by him with a tray.

"Mr Bagthorpe Senior has gone back to sleep," she informed them, "and Mrs Bagthorpe Senior don't want her breakfast. Says she don't think she'll ever want her breakfast again. Two wasted breakfasts."

"Please?" said Jack again, and his mother nodded.

He took Zero along to get him settled in Mrs Bagthorpe's room before leaving.

"You just lie there and act invisible," he told him. "And for heaven's sake don't chew any paper. Right?"

Zero's tail moved in a way that could be interpreted one way or the other, but Jack patted him anyhow, and said, "Good boy!" with great feeling, because he knew that if you trusted people they tended to justify your trust. Mrs Bagthorpe had once explained this to him, and Jack thought the same might apply to dogs.

Uncle Parker picked Jack up just outside the village to reduce the likelihood of his being seen.

"If anyone does say anything, just say I happened to be driving by, and picked you up," Uncle Parker told him. He accelerated with such force that Jack was pressed right back against the seat. "Got to get a move on. Get a good look round this Occult shop before meeting that train."

They did not get a move on for long because they

caught up with another car. There were another three miles of narrow, winding lanes before the main road and dual carriageway.

"Look at that!" exclaimed Uncle Parker disgustedly. "It's always the same! You've only got to get on a stretch of road like this and next thing you know you're sitting on the tail of a perishing Hat!"

Jack said nothing. He was well acquainted with Uncle Parker's theories about other drivers. Uncle Parker put all drivers other than himself into one of various categories, none of them flattering. Rock bottom of these, Jack knew, was the Hat Category.

"The minute you get behind a Hat," Uncle Parker would say, "you know you're finished. Doesn't matter whether it's a man or a woman. And a Flat Cap – you get behind a Flat Cap and you might as well reverse back to where you started and try an alternative route."

He had actually done this once, on this very stretch of road when trapped behind a flat-capped man driving a 1956 Morris Minor. He had reversed at speed for half a mile. Grandma, who had been persuaded to get into the car only with the utmost difficulty in the first place, had screamed the whole way backwards even though her eyes were tightly shut.

"If we are stuck behind a Hat," said Uncle Parker, "we

may as well get some notes written. The speed we are going at," (forty miles per hour) "you could balance a spirit level on your nose, let alone write. Got Prong One?"

"Got it."

"Write:

1. Dowsing rod.
2. Dowsing Instruction Manual.
3. Pack Tarot cards.
4. Incense.
5. Crystal ball."

Jack wrote as directed. Uncle Parker gave a blast on his horn.

"Out, damned Hat!" he muttered under his breath. The passenger seated by the Hat turned and looked round and Uncle Parker made furious waving signals unrecognised by the Green Cross Code, but unmistakably indicating that he wished, urgently, to pass. This evidently annoyed the driver in front because he reduced his speed insufficiently to allow even Uncle Parker to overtake, but sufficiently to aggravate him further. He in turn responded by blasting on his Special Horn and switching on a battery of head and spotlights, a tactic which sometimes worked with Hats, who could, according to Uncle Parker, fall into one of two subdivisions: Nervous or Obstinate. The present Hat must have fallen into the second subdivision because he maintained his speed and gave an answering blast on his horn, though admittedly not one that could be compared with Uncle Parker's, which was an extra he had had fitted for such occasions as this, and sounded roughly like the mating call of a hyena.

"Must be deaf as well as daft," said Uncle Parker. "Got that lot written down?"

"Yes. It sounds smashing. Can just anyone see into a crystal ball?"

"No," returned Uncle Parker. "In fact, nobody can, as far as I know. It's merely a useful prop."

"Oh," said Jack, relieved. It was not that he was scared of *not* being able to see things in the crystal ball, but that he thought he might get scared if he did. "What about Prong Two. What's this Manifestation?"

"Ah..." Again Uncle Parker smiled to himself. "Now as to that, I can't let you in on the whole thing. For one thing, I'm not sure of all the details yet, and for another I haven't had a chance to judge how your acting's going on. You seem to be doing all right, judging by the state you had your father in last night, but this particular Manifestation is going to be a stiff test."

"It sounds marvellous. Can't you give me just a hint?"

"Oh, I can do that. Got to, in fact. Hello – the Hat's turning off!"

The Hat was, indeed, turning into the drive of a small bungalow. On the gate, in large letters, was the legend "DUNROAMIN".

"Ha!" Uncle Parker was triumphant. He was so delighted that he even gave the astonished Hat a grin and cheery wave as he accelerated by.

"See that?"

This was an extension of Uncle Parker's theory. He said that nearly all Hats lived in houses called "Dunroamin" or "Chez Nous" or, at a pinch, "Rose Cottage".

As they streaked on towards Aysham Uncle Parker gave Jack his instructions for initiating Prong Two of the Attack.

"You can use the crystal ball," he said, "or you can look past people's ears, or just at any space that comes in handy. But what you must do, is keep muttering certain Key Words and Phrases."

"Key Words and Phrases," repeated Jack, and efficiently noted them down on the Prong Two page.

"Which are as follows," dictated Uncle Parker, dexterously swerving past a motor cyclist – "look at that fool in front – Where's his indicator? – Does he think I'm clairvoyant?"

The Special Hooter was administered reprovingly as Uncle Parker passed the erring motorist.

"Key Words and Phrases which are as follows… 'from the sky… message from above… Giant Bubble…'"

"Did you say giant bubble? Soap bubble, d'you mean?"

"I said Giant Bubble. Write it down."

Jack wrote it down. He then repeated what he had so far:

"From the sky… message from above… Giant Bubble."

"Anything on those lines," Uncle Parker told him. "Stuff about the heavens opening – anything. Do a bit of improvisation, as long as you stick to the general theme. No details, though – keep it all a bit vague and hazy."

So far as Jack was concerned, it *was* all a bit vague and hazy. He grasped the general theme only dimly and thought it unlikely he would attempt improvisation.

"Oh – I forgot to mention," said Uncle Parker. "The Giant Bubble is red and white. Get that in – just a single telling detail, that's all that's wanted. That's it for now. Got to concentrate."

They were now approaching the outskirts of Aysham. Uncle Parker did, it was true, concentrate on his driving, but what he seemed to be concentrating on was how many narrow shaves he could achieve without actual impact. His concentration was obviously remarkable because the only casualty in all the years Jack had known him had been Thomas. But people were not fair to Uncle Parker. They held his close shaves against him exactly as they would have done actual accidents. The neighbourhood was by now thickly populated by people who had been involved in one of his close shaves, and of course a lot of them recognised his car and pulled in when they saw it coming either towards them or in their rearview mirror.

"It's not so much fun driving round here as it used to be," Uncle Parker told Jack as for the third time a pedestrian put one foot on a zebra, saw Uncle Parker's car approaching and hastily withdrew it.

After the mandatory number of close shaves Uncle Parker finally drew up in a small side street outside a seedy-looking shop. The windows were draped with imitation cobwebs and the centrepiece of the display was a human skull. Above the shop was painted in white dripping candle grease on purple:

MYSTERIES PROP J. E. FERN

"Here we are," said Uncle Parker cheerfully. "Now let's see what we can find."

They spent nearly an hour in the shop. The person who ran it was a white-faced young man with hair that was longer than his beard, and bare feet. When Uncle Parker asked him about his shoes and socks he replied that he did not believe in shoes and socks. He went on for a long time giving his reasons for this, which were apparently something to do with electro-magnetic forces of the earth, but both Jack and Uncle Parker eventually lost interest and began pottering about while J. E. Fern got on with his explanation.

They really enjoyed this. The shop was quite unlike any they had been in before. Uncle Parker kept picking up books, reading bits out to Jack at random, then laughing and pushing them back in the shelves. In the end this must have got on J. E. Fern's nerves because suddenly he said abruptly and in distinctly sepulchral tones:

"You are not, I hope, thinking of dabbling?"

"Dabbling?" queried Uncle Parker.

"In my position," said J. E. Fern, "I have a solemn duty to warn people. The merchandise I offer is essentially for the Believer, for the earnest enquirer into the mysteries of the universe. Hence the name – MYSTERIES."

"Well, I gathered that," conceded Uncle Parker.

"I warn all who enter," continued J. E. Fern, "that to dabble is not only unwise, it is positively dangerous."

Jack thought that J. E. Fern looked as if he led a pretty haunted life himself, and began to wonder if perhaps they should opt out while it was still open to them.

"I give you my word," said Uncle Parker, "that one thing

I never do is dabble. Young Jack here will bear me out. If I do a thing I do it thoroughly. Now, you're obviously a chap who has gone into this whole thing thoroughly. Tell me, what advice would you give us as beginners? Not dabblers, you understand, those who wish to learn."

Uncle Parker could get round most people when he made the effort. In no time at all he had J. E. Fern eating out of his hand and he even ended up by letting him have a crystal ball (which was exorbitantly priced) on a seven-day-trial basis, deposit refunded if not entirely satisfied. Jack himself fervently hoped that the crystal ball would not give satisfaction, and not just because of the price. He felt much the same way as Grandma and Tess did about visitations.

As well as the crystal ball they bore away a dowsing rod plus manual, some mixed incense sticks which the man said were very conducive to Visions and Jack privately resolved to burn only during the daytime, and some Tarot cards which looked interesting, if sinister.

When they left J. E. Fern's, Uncle Parker shot up another street and fetched two cream buns from a shop and they sat companionably munching them on a solid yellow line.

"One last thing," said Uncle Parker. "The money. We'll get our deposit back on the crystal ball – we only need it for a week or so just to put the fear of God into them. The rest you pay for."

"I didn't really want a dowsing rod and incense," Jack said.

"I can't buy them for you," Uncle Parker told him. "They'd rumble us the minute they found out. In any case, I think you ought to invest in the Campaign to show good faith."

"It'll take every penny I've got outside the Savings Bank," said Jack bleakly.

"I know how much it cost," said Uncle Parker. "I paid it, remember. You pay me back first chance you get."

"All right," Jack said.

"It is, of course, your birthday in six weeks' time," mused Uncle Parker. "No telling what I couldn't slip you on that felicitous occasion."

"Oh, *thanks*," said Jack gratefully. "You see, I was saving up for this model glider."

Uncle Parker shook his head.

"You're far too normal, that's your trouble," he told him. "Any of the others, they'd be saving up for a Stradivarius or some records to teach themselves Swahili. Lord – that reminds me – look at the time. Out – quick! Here – your parcel."

Jack had been about to leave it on the back seat of the car.

"I'll have to race like hell," said Uncle Parker with satisfaction, already revving.

"And watch how you carry that crystal ball!" he yelled out of the window, to the interest of passers-by. "It's not a cabbage, you know!"

Gingerly Jack made his way to the bus stop. It seemed to him that if a crystal ball really did have the magic properties described by J. E. Fern, it would be courting disaster to drop it. It would also, of course, cost him the best part of a year's pocket money.

Chapter Nine

WHEN JACK REACHED home the house was unusually quiet. It had the air of a place in which a lot of people are lying low. Mrs Fosdyke was busy enough in the kitchen, however, and lunch was definitely on.

"Where is everybody?" he enquired.

"The Lord knows why," replied Mrs Fosdyke at a tangent, "Mrs Bagthorpe had to send for that chit in the first place. I've always tried to give satisfaction. There's never been any complaints."

Mrs Fosdyke had been tactfully told of the *au pair*'s impending arrival some weeks previously by Mrs Bagthorpe. She had simply been told that the main reason for the visit was to bring Tess's Danish on, and to have someone to help with the driving and perhaps do the odd chore.

Mrs Fosdyke had not been convinced by this. She did not say so to Mrs Bagthorpe, but in the Fiddler's Arms she said what she really felt, which was that the whole thing was casting aspersions on herself, and could even be the first step towards her herself being made ultimately redundant.

"They'll find their mistake, of course," she said. "I've seen one or two films with them Danish orpairs and it's not chores they do, oh dear me no."

Jack was wise enough not to pursue the matter of the new arrival.

"Is Zero still in Mother's room?" he asked.

Mrs Fosdyke, on the other hand, was not prepared to let the matter go.

"Up in her room," she said. "Been up there ever since she got here. Weeping buckets."

"Crying? What for?"

Mrs Fosdyke shrugged her shoulders.

"These Continentals is all the same. I've seen some of them subtitle films. It's no surprise to me."

Jack decided against going to Mrs Bagthorpe's room to check on Zero in case he interrupted a Problem. He filled in the time until lunch by going to his room and unwrapping his parcel from MYSTERIES. After a quick look at the crystal ball he put it back in its straw-packed box in case he should accidentally happen to glance at it and see something in there. There was not much he could do with the dowsing gear, so he lit a jasmine-scented stick of incense and stuck it in a half-finished scone he had brought up the previous night. He watched the tiny red tip of the stick and the thinly wreathing smoke and soon the scent reached him. He sniffed. He rather liked it. He sniffed again. After that he tried to breathe ordinarily because it might, it occurred to him, be the deliberate inhaling of the incense that brought the Visions on. He even got up and opened a window.

"If Zero doesn't like the smell I shan't burn it in here anyway," he decided.

He lay on his bed studying the book that accompanied the Tarot cards. The whole thing seemed very complicated. There was little doubt that any futures Jack foretold would be based upon pure guesswork, with or without the benefit of the Tarot cards.

There was a tap on his door and his mother and Zero came in together. The latter leapt on the bed and licked Jack's face, then jumped off and stood by the scone with the incense stick in it, sniffing rapturously.

"There's a queer smell in here," began Mrs Bagthorpe, "and what—"

She noticed the incense stick and Zero. She took a deep breath and Jack knew this meant she was going to be very calm and reasonable despite strong urges to be the opposite. It was part of her Yoga.

"Quite a nice smell," she said determinedly forcing a slight smile. "Jasmine, isn't it?"

He nodded.

"There's several flavours," he told her. "Sandalwood and amber and rose and stuff."

"Was that what you went into Aysham for?" she asked. "Or perhaps you went for that model glider you're saving up for?"

"I'm going to wait before I buy that," he said. "There are more things in heaven and earth than gliders and I had to spend my money on priorities."

"Which are...?"

"These –" he waved the Tarot pack – "and those!"

He jerked his head towards the dowsing rod and the box containing the crystal ball. The box said CRYSTAL BALL FIRST QUALITY on it, so she could see at a glance what it was. She sat down suddenly.

"Sometimes," she said, half to herself, "I think I ought to give up other people's Problems and concentrate on my own. I think I fail you."

"You mustn't worry about me, Mother." Jack could not

help feeling guilty. He wanted to be a Phenomenon and a Prophet all right, but not if it was going to upset her too much. "I expect it's just a passing phase I'm going through."

She clutched gratefully at this straw.

"Yes, I expect that's it. After all, you're a growing boy. You're bound to have passing phases."

"I think everyone gets them sometimes," said Jack wisely. He was enjoying this unaccustomed philosophical discussion. "Probably you do as well."

"Do you know, I think I do," she agreed.

"And Grandma certainly does," said Jack with conviction.

"Oh dear – and that's another thing. She's still in bed. Oh, and that Danish girl – such a commotion."

"Mrs Fosdyke said she was crying when she got here," Jack said. "Perhaps it was Uncle Parker's driving that had upset her. It can be pretty frightening if you're not used to it."

"Do you know, that's exactly what your father said. He said it was enough to reduce anyone to tears. You know how he talks – but he could be right."

"How is he?" asked Jack.

"Oh, and that's another thing. He's like a caged beast. He's up and dressed now and pacing round and round his study. It must be terrible to have all that creativity bottled up inside you. I don't think any of us realise what he suffers."

"Zero probably does," said Jack. "Zero suffers a lot."

"And of course Tess is dreadfully upset," continued Mrs Bagthorpe on her own tack. "You know how she was looking forward to Atlanta coming."

"Atlanta!" said Jack scornfully. He felt much the same as Grandma did about this name, and Mrs Fosdyke had already flatly stated that she was not calling anybody by that name, ever.

"She doesn't seem to understand much English, either," went on Mrs Bagthorpe worriedly. "I understood that she was more or less bilingual."

It later transpired that Mrs Bagthorpe's fears were justified. Atlanta was, indeed, bilingual, but the languages involved were Danish and Portuguese. Her command of English was negligible. It did not even amount, as Mr Bagthorpe said, to a smattering. She could say "please" and "sank you" and "yes" and "no". She could also say, "Plees haf you change for a pound," and, "I haf an aunt who lifs in Bournemouth," and count up to ten. None of which, he further pointed out, was going to take her far in the English social scene.

As it turned out, Atlanta did not need to speak English in order to become the centre of a social whirl. All she needed to do was appear. She was, once she had stopped crying and the swelling of her eyes and nose had subsided, devastating. She was Mrs Fosdyke's worst fears come true, the prototype of every Danish *au pair* she had ever seen in films.

At this stage, of course, none of this had emerged. As yet the Bagthorpes knew only that they had a seventeen-year-old Danish girl with a blotchy face sobbing her heart out in the guest room and not seeming to understand a word that was said to her. Next door Tess was crying too, but not so noisily.

"Jack, dear –" Mrs Bagthorpe rose. "Could you go along and see if your grandparents want lunch? I shall have to go and have another word with Atlanta."

Grandpa wanted lunch but Grandma refused, saying she didn't want any lunch and didn't feel as if she ever would again. Atlanta stayed in her room and Tess stayed in hers in sympathy. Jack felt annoyed with Atlanta before he had even set eyes on her. She was disrupting a household he had been all set to disrupt himself. At the moment it did not seem as if there was going to be room for both of them.

Mr Bagthorpe was at his bitterest at lunch. He had not written a single word that morning, not even a page or two he could tear up, which was in fact all he did some days.

"Not that it matters, of course," he said, chasing peas left-handed round his plate. "The English language will soon become extinct. There are already signs of it. I shall see it in my lifetime."

"Nonsense, dear," said his wife.

"Even my own children reject it in favour of debased and hybrid continental lingos," he went on. "Why did you say that girl was crying?"

"I didn't," she told him. "None of us can find out."

"If she's got hysteria as a result of being driven in Russell's car, she'll have to get over it as best she can," he said. "Take aspirin or something. I'm not having that doctor in my house again."

"Had any Visions or anything this morning?" William asked Jack, changing the subject before Mr Bagthorpe took right off. Jack pretended not to hear. It suddenly occurred to him that if he pretended not to hear half the things that were said to him, particularly if they were awkward or sarcastic things, this would create the impression that he was in Another World in a very painless and effective way.

"I'm getting on quite well with my portrait of Grandma," Rosie said, contributing her bit towards the brisk and lively interchange of ideas and opinions that was supposed to characterise Bagthorpe mealtimes. "It's much easier without her there."

"Lovely, darling," said Mrs Bagthorpe encouragingly. Then, "Mother hasn't eaten a thing all day," she told her husband.

"That doesn't surprise me," he returned. "I'm having to force my own food down. After what's gone on in this house in the last forty-eight hours nothing would surprise me, not any longer. It wouldn't surprise me if the heavens opened and it began to hail mothballs."

Startled, Jack recognised a totally unexpected cue, a real bonus, and from his father, of all people.

"... the heavens opening..." he murmured, fixing his eyes on the remainder of his lamb chop. "The sky..." he fumbled for the third Key Phrase, and found it – "... a Giant Bubble..."

"Oh my God, here we go again!" Mr Bagthorpe flung down his fork and his peas scattered.

"I have made up my mind," came Grandma's voice unexpectedly, "that I shall take up Yoga."

Everyone at the table, with the exception of Grandpa, turned towards the door.

"You – will – do – what?" Mr Bagthorpe left quite a long space between each word, which was a bad sign with him. It meant his control was running out.

"There's no need to space your words out at me like that," Grandma told him. "I'm perfectly *compos mentis*, thank you."

"In that case," said her son, "you're about the only person left round here who is. You're *what*?"

"For someone who is supposed to be a writer," said his mother, purposely ignoring the question, "you don't use the language at all well. You have no grace of expression."

Grandma could usually rely on a good argument with her son when she really felt like one, and was now in her goading stage. Once goaded, he was usually a match for her.

"Look at this! Look!" Mr Bagthorpe waved his solid white arm above the table. "Do you know what this means?"

"It means," returned Grandma, "that you were silly enough, at your age, to attempt a headstand in order to show off, and that you reaped your just deserts."

"We'll leave personalities out of it, if you don't mind," said Mr Bagthorpe, who was a fine one to talk. "That was an objective question I asked you. This, Mother, is a broken limb."

"So I understand." She sat now in the rocker, which made an irritating creak when she rocked it.

"Just the one limb," said Mr Bagthorpe, waving it again. "Now, if you take up Yoga – and I still wonder whether I heard you aright – you will break all your limbs. You will break every limb in your body, or fracture it. You will end up, in fact, looking like a replica of an Egyptian mummy."

"Thank you," said Grandma calmly.

"Your face might perhaps show," he added, "but that'd be all."

"I have been Breathing all morning, you know," said Grandma, addressing herself to Mrs Bagthorpe now, in the certain knowledge that this would goad Mr Bagthorpe still further.

"Lovely, Mother," said Mrs Bagthorpe encouragingly.

"Unavoidable, I should have thought," said Mr Bagthorpe.

"I have been reading one of your books, Laura," Grandma went on. "In many ways I think it would be a good thing if we all took up Yoga. The whole family."

"Tess is certainly interested," agreed Mrs Bagthorpe.

"I wouldn't mind trying," piped up Rosie.

"Now, listen here," said Mr Bagthorpe, abandoning his peas and beginning to gnaw his chop while holding it in his left hand. "If I am going to be driven beyond human endurance for the next few weeks, as I undoubtedly am, with my right hand in hock, if all you lot are going to sit around all day looking blissful and Breathing, I'm getting out. I shall just clear out."

"But it would be an ideal time for you to take it up too, dear," said Mrs Bagthorpe unwisely. "What do you think, Mother?"

This was the point at which Grandma's goading paid

off. Mr Bagthorpe smelled, he said, a conspiracy. It was a conspiracy, moreover, to make him into what he called "a creative eunuch", though nobody knew what he meant by this. If he had been born to sit around breathing, or lying on his back with his legs folded in the air, then he thought that by now he would have discovered this vocation for himself. He further thought it unlikely that anyone would pay him for doing this, while at the present the BBC, however unwisely in the eyes of his own family and so-called friends, were paying him very high prices for his scripts – above the going rates. Which was lucky, he said, for the lot of them, who would not now be sitting stuffing themselves with lamb cutlets and living generally off the fat of the land were it not for his prodigious creative output. And so on, and so on…

Jack, sitting forgotten, his Giant Bubble quite pricked, could see Grandma's entrance at that particular moment only as a form of miracle – of the intervention, at any rate, of some kind of Higher Power. The present tirade would undoubtedly have been directed at himself and Zero had it not been for her timely arrival.

His Bubble did have a comeback of sorts later in the day, however, when the furore had died down. Not that any furore ever quite died down – the Bagthorpes lived, one might say, in a perpetual state of simmer. Luckily, they all thrived on it, with the exception, perhaps, of Jack, though even he was beginning to feel the adrenalin flow, to taste the delights of living dangerously.

The way the Giant Bubble came up again was this. After lunch Jack crept off, fetched Zero from his room and slunk out the back way. He did not escape the eye of Mrs Fosdyke because he had to nip stealthily into the kitchen to fill his pockets with biscuits, the ones Zero liked. He was spotted in the act. He moved off sharply.

"Where are you off to?" she called after him, but he pretended he had not heard. He was beginning to discover too the advantages of being SD.

Where Jack was off to was a small, private meadow he knew of, one with plenty of maythorn thickets and high, waving hedges. The reason he was going there was because he was positive that the previous day he had achieved a breakthrough with Zero in the stick-fetching business. There had been something about the look in Zero's eyes, for that fraction of a second after Jack had finally ducked down and come up with the stick between his teeth. The look he had caught had, he felt certain, been dawning comprehension, or, at the very least, a glimmer.

Jack realised that if he wished to pursue his career as a Prophet and Phenomenon he must never be observed, especially by any of the Bagthorpes, with a stick between his teeth. (He was no longer afraid of committal to an asylum. From the things Dr Winters had said the previous evening, if anyone got committed, it would be Mr Bagthorpe.)

The little meadow was still and sunlit and patched with dandelions and cow parsley and seeded plantain. It seemed a forgotten place. Jack never saw anyone there. He lay on his back in the warm grass for a while. He had managed a substantial lunch while the others were having their furore. Zero too slumped in the shade of a maythorn and dozed. At length, reluctantly, Jack pulled himself up.

"Come on, Zero," he said. "Good boy. We're going to play Fetch."

Zero lifted his head and thumped his tail.

"And this time," Jack told him, "*you're* going to Fetch. Get it? Not me. *You*. Good *boy*."

Zero's tail thumped harder than Jack had ever seen it. Jack knew that this was a crucial moment, a turning point. He had a sudden inspiration.

"We'll have a race," he told Zero. "See who fetches it first. I'll throw the stick, then we'll see who can pick it up first. Right?"

From the way Zero was dancing and wagging his tail Jack would have sworn he had understood, word for word.

Jack held the stick high.

"Ready?" he cried, then, "Fetch!"

He dropped instantly on to all fours and began to scramble hell for leather in the direction he had thrown, and the next thing he knew he was face to face with a panting, prancing Zero with *the stick held between his teeth.*

Very slowly Jack rose to his knees. He stared, awestruck, into Zero's hopeful brown eyes.

"Oh, good *boy*!" he managed. "Oh, good *boy*," but he hardly did manage it because tears, ridiculously, were stinging his eyes and choking up his voice. He reached into his pocket and wordlessly held out a handful of Grannie's Cookies and Zero, after a moment's hesitation, dropped the stick and wolfed them down. As he did so Jack was patting his tousled fur, stroking his head.

"Oh, *Zero*," he said. "You *good* boy. I told you. I knew you could do it. Good boy. Good old boy."

The two of them spent a long, happy afternoon in the meadow. By the end of it there was no need for Jack to get down on all fours himself, there was no need even for him to reward Zero with biscuits (which had run out, anyhow). All he had to do was stand there, shout, "Fetch, Zero!" and hurl the stick. Within sixty seconds flat the stick would be back in his hand.

"Right," he told Zero at last. "And now we are going to show that lot what's what."

He walked back over the fields with a new spring in

his step. Zero walked ahead and it seemed to Jack there was a spring in *his* step now, as well, and his ears had pricked up almost unrecognisably. Jack marched straight into the sitting-room and announced without ceremony,

"I've got something I want you all to see. All come out here a minute."

The assembled Bagthorpes, and as it so happened, they were all assembled, literally boggled at him. The ring of his voice was something quite new. Was this ordinary Jack, Jack with no Strings to his Bow, Jack who seemed only by some freak of nature to be a Bagthorpe? So stunned were they that they obeyed, without question. Even Mr Bagthorpe levered himself out of his chair and followed the others, albeit muttering inaudibly under his breath.

"All right, everybody."

Jack turned and faced them.

"Now you're going to see something."

"The heavens opening?" enquired Mr Bagthorpe, not sufficiently nonplussed to have lost his usual style.

"No," said Jack. "Not the heavens opening. Something better."

He lifted the stick he held in his hand and Zero sat panting, his gaze fixed on it.

"Oh no!" he heard his father exclaim. "Not that again. I can't stand it!"

Then, "Fetch, Zero!" Jack yelled, and hurled the stick as hard as he could.

All you could hear was the thudding of Zero's paws on the turf and then, as he returned, stick between his teeth, his panting. Jack bent and took the stick from him. He patted Zero's head.

"Good boy," he said. Again he felt his voice tremble. "Good old boy."

He turned then and faced the family.

"Well?" he demanded. "What about that?"

"My sainted aunt!" he heard his father say. "There *will* be a Giant Bubble. It's a miracle. It's a ruddy miracle!"

And then, all at once, the Bagthorpes were in a tumult of delight and congratulation. They patted and praised Zero – they almost patted and praised Jack. They were, to a man, hugely and genuinely delighted.

Jack, still a little dazed and shaken, stood and let it all ebb and flow about him, and thought:

They mean it. They're really glad. I can't believe it. Oh, good old Zero, good old boy!

Chapter Ten

By the following day things had calmed down a little. Mrs Bagthorpe had discovered what was the matter with Atlanta. It had been a combination of Uncle Parker's driving, and homesickness. Mrs Bagthorpe had made these discoveries in two parts. She had given an imitation of someone driving a car, at the same time making a brum-brumming noise, at which Atlanta had nodded her head vigorously and redoubled her sobs. Then, while helping her unpack Mrs Bagthorpe had come upon a photograph album which Atlanta had instantly seized upon, turning the pages while tears splashed on to the smiling faces of her family.

Mrs Bagthorpe was relieved by these findings, which

were, after all, only healthy and natural. At least there would be no need to call the doctor. She did not really want to call him again for as long as possible. She knew, of course, that members of the medical profession were not supposed to bear grudges against patients, but could see how Dr Winters was being sorely tempted in this particular instance.

Mrs Bagthorpe had comforted Atlanta, and Tess came in and bashfully spoke a few Danish words, and thus she had finally been settled. Next morning she emerged transformed. She swung into the kitchen where various members of the family were at different stages of breakfasting.

"Ello," she said.

"Hello," they chorused, all turning.

"Oh. Hello." It was William's voice putting in an extra greeting. Jack looked at him in surprise. For an instant he wondered whether William had decided to go into the Mysterious Impressions business, so strange and staring did he look. Jack sincerely hoped not. He did not want the competition, and in any case, if anyone stared past this girl's ear it might set her off crying for hours on end again. Jack had already made a mental note to give her a miss, along with Grandma and Mr Bagthorpe.

"Do sit down, dear," said Mrs Bagthorpe, indicating her place. William leapt up and pulled the chair out and the rest of the family gaped. The Bagthorpes were quite polite in a way, but never excessively so.

She smiled at William.

"Sank you," she said.

"Oh, it's a pleasure," he assured her fervently. He was still looking at her, even now it was sideways on. Luckily Mr Bagthorpe did not notice this because he was too busy trying to butter his toast left-handed. Mr Bagthorpe would not have been able to stand it if another member of his family had started giving Mysterious Impressions.

Jack noticed that Mrs Fosdyke was leaning up against the sink having a good stare at the new arrival too. He himself took another quick look just to see if he could make out why they were looking at her like this. The only thing he could think of was that she did look a *little* bit like Aunt Celia, but not all that much. Not enough to knock anybody sideways.

"Now, what about some breakfast?" asked Mrs Bagthorpe. She had already told the others that they must speak to Atlanta exactly as if she could understand every word.

"You may perhaps speak a little more slowly," she said, "and of course, if necessary, you must point at things and name them to her, as you would with a young child."

None of the Bagthorpes other than Tess had been much pleased by this prospect, but had agreed to do so when

Mrs Bagthorpe had pointed out that the sooner Atlanta picked up some English, the easier it would be for all of them.

"The other alternative," she had said, "is for *us* all to learn Danish –" which had clinched it.

"I'll make some more toast," said Mrs Fosdyke, managing to make this apparently simple offer sound like an insult. "I hope she won't be coming down late every morning."

Mrs Bagthorpe pointed to the toast rack and said clearly: "Some toast, Atlanta?"

"Oh, *ja, ja*." She stretched and took a piece.

"Butter?" It was William, pointing to that commodity.

She smiled sideways at him past her swinging hair, and took it.

"Toast," repeated Mrs Bagthorpe firmly, "and butter."

She pointed again. Atlanta got the message.

"Toast," she repeated, "and butter."

It was very good except that she missed the 't' off the end of toast and pronounced the 'u' of butter as in 'good'.

"She said it!" cried William admiringly.

Jack took another look at him. If he were not going in for Mysterious Impressions, then clearly what was happening was that Atlanta was making a very mysterious impression on him.

"She don't pronounce very well," observed Mrs Fosdyke.

This was just one of the drawbacks of having the dining room burnt out – Mrs Fosdyke chipped into conversations a lot more often. William turned and gave her a quelling look.

"Perhaps you'd like to say toast and butter in Danish for us?" he enquired scathingly.

"William!" reproved his mother.

Mrs Fosdyke drew herself up, looked for a moment as if she might be going to say something (though almost certainly not toast and butter in Danish) then turned her back and began rattling things in the sink. She had a special way she could rattle if she wanted to, and was doing it now. Mr Bagthorpe gave up trying to turn the pages of his newspaper one-handed and glowered at her back. He muttered something that Jack did not catch but that definitely contained the word "hedgehog".

At this point Zero, who had not met Atlanta the previous day, got up, walked to her, and wagged his tail. She turned delightedly and patted his head and said something that was evidently the Danish for "Good boy" because he wagged his tail all the more. Zero, thought Jack with satisfaction, evidently understood Danish better than any of them.

"Dog," said Jack boldly, and pointed at Zero. "Dog. Name Zero."

"Dorg. Name Sero," she said.

"It's incredible," William said. "She picks up everything you say."

Mr Bagthorpe opened his mouth and then closed it again in much the same way as Mrs Fosdyke just had. He had, Jack guessed, been about to say something about keeping that mutton-headed hound out of his way, and then changed his mind. He had, after all, in front of witnesses, been proved totally mistaken in his assessment of Zero's intellectual capabilities. Jack himself had always known Zero was not stupid, and this morning had deliberately brought him down instead of leaving him up in his room as usual. He felt it was now time he took his rightful place in the household.

Jack realised that today he was on his own. There had been no early morning conference with Uncle Parker in the dew, and there would be no rendezvous in a fast-moving car. He did not particularly care whether he progressed much today. He felt that he and Zero could rest on their laurels for a while after yesterday's performance. The Bagthorpes had already been treated to one display of the Phenomenal.

This was where he made his mistake. He naturally assumed that Zero would, from now on, be a name synonymous with hero. He was wrong. The whole point of being a member of the Bagthorpe *ménage* was that you never, but never, rested on any laurels.

He began to discover this after he had been throwing Zero sticks to fetch for nearly an hour on the lawn at the front of the house. He had not taken into account that the house at present contained some very jumpy people, and that jumpy people have nerves which are very easily grated upon.

The first of them was Mrs Fosdyke, who happened to be cleaning the inside of the front windows, probably to let off her feelings. She thumped on a window several times with a duster to indicate that she was not enjoying the performance, but Jack mistook this as a sign of appreciation, a kind of improvised applause of the stamping of feet variety. In the end she flung open the window.

"I can't be doing with this rumpus all morning!" she shouted above Zero's excited barking.

"I thought you'd like to see him do it," Jack called back. "You've never actually seen him, have you?"

"Heard enough about it," she said. "And now I've seen him. Very nice. I'll go and do the windows round the back."

And so, presumably she did. She certainly disappeared.

Grandma was the next objector. She too threw open a window – that of her own bedroom. Jack looked up.

"Do you realise," she called, "that I am trying to Breathe?"

"Oh. I'm sorry. I didn't realise."

"I can't Breathe with that noise going on," she said. "You have to concentrate. And if I am to survive much longer in this household then it is vital I go on breathing."

"Yes," agreed Jack. "I'm sorry, Grandma. I'll go and do it round the back. Come on, Zero."

The first thing he encountered round the back was Mrs Fosdyke's face grimacing at him through a window behind a large duster.

"Come on, Zero," he said.

They went right to the very edge of the garden, where it met the meadow. There the two of them started up again, but the game was not to last for long.

"For pity's sake!" shouted a familiar voice. "Is there *no* peace to be had?"

Jack turned about, uncertain where the voice had come from.

"I may as well give up," came Mr Bagthorpe's gloomy voice.

Jack spotted him. He was only head and shoulders visible in the long grass of the meadow, through which could be seen glimpses of the thick, snow-white arm amongst the green.

"I didn't know you were there," he shouted. "Sorry!"

Mr Bagthorpe sank slowly out of sight like a submarine

submerging. Jack wondered what he was doing. His father never lay around in meadows. He felt that simply to go through the wicket gate and peer would look merely inquisitive. He needed an excuse to go in there, and a solution immediately struck him. He raised the stick, threw it as hard as he could in the approximate position Mr Bagthorpe had last been seen, and shouted:

"Fetch!"

With this he flung open the wicket and Zero thundered past with Jack in hot pursuit. He was pulled up by a bloodcurdling yell of rage and despair. Jack, who was used to ordinary kinds of yell, stopped dead in his tracks. Mr Bagthorpe surfaced again right by Zero, and seemed to be lunging after him.

Zero, probably temporarily unhinged by the terrible cry, instead of returning to Jack as usual, veered right off track across the meadow in the opposite direction. It looked to Jack as if he had something else in his mouth besides the stick. He raced right to the far side of the meadow and then must have lain down because all at once he disappeared. He was probably chewing the stick, Jack thought, because he was nervous. Jack knew just how he felt. Sometimes his own nails were down to the quick.

Mr Bagthorpe, astonishingly, was lurching over the meadow in the direction Zero had taken. He was yelling loudly. Jack could not hear all of it, but all the old catch-phrases were there among it – "mutton-brained" and "useless" and "godawful beast".

Jack followed at a fast rate. He and his father were just about level when Zero became visible, lying on the trodden-down footpath by the hedge. He was chewing and snorting as he had done the day he caught a rat. (He only once ever caught a rat, and Mr Bagthorpe had said that it must obviously have been dead already, and Zero just happened to find it.)

What Zero was chewing now looked like a kind of long black worm with a large head, though Jack had certainly never observed a creature of this nature in the meadow before.

"Ruination!" cried Mr Bagthorpe in anguish. "My last link with sanity snapped!"

He actually clutched at his head, Jack heard the bump of plaster cast against his skullbone. He was going to have to learn to make fewer such gestures. Jack raced to get to Zero ahead of him. Zero was still growling and worrying whatever it was in his mouth. Jack's heart dropped like a stone. He could not see exactly what it was in Zero's jaws, but trailing from it was a long black length of flex with a two-pronged plug at the end of it.

Mr Bagthorpe was for once lost for words. He just stood

there for a while and groaned and beat his forehead with his good hand. When he did finally speak, it was only to repeat himself:

"My last link with sanity – snapped!"

Jack knelt by Zero and held out his hand.

"Give, Zero," he commanded. "Give. Good boy!"

"Good boy!" yelled Mr Bagthorpe. "What d'you mean good boy? Hound of hell!"

Zero dropped what he had in his mouth into Jack's hand and slouched off alongside the hedge with his tail down. Jack looked down at what he held. It felt rough and damp – it had once been smooth and dry. It was the microphone of a tape recorder – chewed out of existence.

"If I should go mad," said Mr Bagthorpe dully, "think only this of me. I was a man hounded out of my mind."

He turned and began to drag away back over the meadow, his white arm hanging loosely by his side. If his ears had been the drooping kind, they would have been drooping. Jack was torn between feeling sorry for him and sorry for Zero. He felt sorry for them both. He decided to leave the former alone, for the time being, and set off after the latter, to have a few reproachful words with him.

He felt that Zero could not be held wholly responsible for the tragedy because he could not, in all fairness, have expected to find an exciting-looking snake tangled up with his stick and was naturally excited when he did so. Jack felt that if his father had wished to dictate his scripts into a cassette recorder he should have done it in the obvious place, his study, or else given everyone fair warning that he would be concealed in the long grass doing it.

Even so, he wondered whether he ought to offer to buy a new microphone. The trouble with this idea was that he already owed all his spare cash to Uncle Parker for the MYSTERIES.

"And a lot of good they've done me," he reflected.

Once Jack had given the matter some thought, however, he could see how it had all come about. What had really been at the bottom of it all, was false pride – Mr Bagthorpe's. One of his favourite topics was the inefficiency, hatefulness and general destructiveness of machines in any form. (He conveniently ignored the fact that his own livelihood depended on one of these obnoxious devices – namely, the television.) The only machine he would have any truck with was his typewriter, and even that was so old that it could hardly be called a machine. It was more of a makeshift. It was over thirty years old and the BBC were always ringing up to check words it had mistyped. Mr Bagthorpe saw this as a virtue. It showed, he said, that the typewriter had a mind of its own, and was something to be reckoned with.

"Machines," he was fond of saying, "are the opium of

the masses. If all the machines in England were thrown into the North Sea tomorrow, we should be back in the Garden of Eden. And the weather would probably improve."

Nobody ever argued with him, except Grandma, sometimes, when she felt like it. The rest of them went cheerfully on using their electronic devices, electric guitars and dishwashers, and so on, without a moral misgiving in the world.

Mrs Bagthorpe had given her husband a portable cassette recorder for Christmas some years ago. She recognised that she was playing with fire, but decided to risk it, especially as it was the season of goodwill and Mr Bagthorpe really did try to keep calm and kind over Christmas.

He had thanked her for it in a formal kind of way and put it in a cupboard where it had been ever since. Once or twice over the years Mrs Bagthorpe had timidly suggested that he might use it occasionally, to capture his dialogue.

"The day I speak my thoughts into any machine," he had said (almost prophetically, as it turned out), "will be the day my right arm is cut off."

Or, alternatively:

"Can you imagine William Shakespeare dictating *Othello* into one of those things? Did Keats use one? Or Dickens? Or Tolstoy?"

To which there was no answer, except the obvious one that these particular writers did not even have the option. Nobody made this point. If you were up against one of Mr Bagthorpe's prejudices you were up against a stone wall. He got it from Grandma.

Now Mr Bagthorpe was faced with the alternative of using the recorder or else doing nothing at all for the next few weeks. He had obviously come round to the idea that he must use the machine, however infernal. He did not, however, wish the family to know this, because he was not good at climbing down. His stock, he must have felt, was already low. He had been wrong about being able to do a headstand, and he had been proved wrong in front of witnesses about Zero being able to fetch sticks. A third public humiliation might loosen his grip on the household altogether. Mr Bagthorpe simply could not afford to be seen to be fallible three times in a row.

Accordingly, he had sneaked out with the recorder under his good arm and concealed himself in the long grass of the meadow to unburden his thoughts. (Jack later got a sight of the cassette in question. It had written on it, with true Bagthorpian modesty: GREAT THOUGHTS: DO NOT ERASE.) Mr Bagthorpe had, he said, been getting nicely into his stride at the point where Jack and Zero had intervened.

Jack and Zero stayed in the fields all morning and so Mr Bagthorpe got his side of the story in first. He had obviously elaborated it a little, and that, combined with his crippled state, had enlisted the sympathy of the rest of the Bagthorpes, who were in any case feeling threatened by Jack's claims to Prophetic status. Grandma was the only one on Jack's side, and it was obvious even to him that this was because she was being cross-grained – a clear indication that her breathing had not done much for her so far.

"How *could* you, Jack?" Mrs Bagthorpe exclaimed reproachfully as he slunk into lunch, having safely ensconced Zero in his bedroom again, to guard the pile of comics.

"I didn't do it on purpose," Jack said. "I'm sorry. I really am. It was a terrible thing to happen."

"A terrible thing to happen, he says," said Mr Bagthorpe, staring dully at his stew. (Mrs Bagthorpe was trying to organise meals that could be eaten with a fork only.) "It's the end of me."

"Nonsense, Henry," said his wife. "It's just a minor setback. I shall take both yourself and Father into Aysham this afternoon and he shall be fitted for a new aid, and you shall choose a new microphone."

"Don't you put me in the same category with him," said Mr Bagthorpe ungratefully. "I'm not completely helpless yet, thank you."

"Atlanta and I are getting on beautifully," Tess now said. "Aren't – we – Atlanta?"

Atlanta nodded and smiled and said, "*Ja, ja*, beautiful," and William stared at her with a forkful of stew halfway to his mouth.

"Why don't we get a muzzle for that hellhound while we're at it?" Mr Bagthorpe rarely listened to anyone else's brisk and lively interchange of views and opinions. "Now he can fetch sticks, which for Pete's sake so can any other dog in England, he's worse than when he couldn't. It's gone to his head. God knows what he'll fetch next if he's not curbed."

"Perhaps you could look into your little crystal ball and tell us?" said William to Jack.

"How do you know about that?"

"Saw it," replied William. "Your room's not sacrosanct, you know. And pooh – what a smell in there!"

"How extremely rude of you," Grandma told William, "to go and pry into Jack's private belongings. Jack, dear, I believe you have some incense sticks. Could you lend me one or two possibly? I have read about them somewhere and feel sure they would help me with my breathing."

"Of course," Jack said gratefully, not even quibbling about how anyone could repay a burnt-out incense stick. "You can choose whichever flavours you like."

"Thank you, dear. And Rosie, if you haven't filled in the background of my Portrait, could you perhaps paint me breathing with an incense stick burning each side of me?"

"I've done the burnt-up dining-room," said Rosie. "You said you wanted to be done in there. And I think it'll make it stand out."

"Could you not *add* the sticks?" persisted Grandma. "It would be very effective to have the smoke swirling mysteriously about me. And this may be my last Portrait. I think my wishes should be respected."

"I suppose so," said Rosie. "I'll try."

In the end five of them went to Aysham that afternoon. William had somehow managed to intimate to Atlanta that he would like to show her round the historic castle there. They drove off, with Mr Bagthorpe muttering something about it being a relief to get out of that house, and leaving Tess to sulk because there had been no room for her to go too. She went off to her room and banged the door loudly. Grandma went up to have a nap. Rosie set off across the meadow towards the village for a swim. She went with Mrs Fosdyke, whose half-day it was. Jack watched them go, wondering whatever they would find to say to one another.

The house was very quiet. Jack went up to his room, where Zero was lying by the pile of comics with his ears drooping again.

"It was rotten luck, old chap," Jack told him, patting him, and feeling sorry now that he had reproached him earlier on. "And at least you're not sly. It's pretty sly to go hiding in long grass talking into microphones."

Zero wagged his tail feebly. Jack felt depressed too. The victory of yesterday had already turned to ashes. At a stroke, it seemed, it had become a defeat.

It's no good, Jack thought. *If I want to make any impression round here, I'll have to press on with the Prophet and Phenomenon thing.*

He was almost tempted to take out the crystal ball. He just did not quite dare risk it. He took out the Tarot cards and played idly with them for a while, but didn't feel that anything special was happening. He remembered that he had pulled in not one Vision or Mysterious Impression all day. He felt thoroughly discouraged and in need of moral support.

I could ring Uncle Parker, he thought. Both telephones were clear, with Mr Bagthorpe and Mrs Fosdyke safely out of the way. But this scheme was still not without its dangers. If either Daisy or Aunt Celia were to answer the telephone, the consequences could be awful. Uncle Parker might wash his hands of him for ever, and he would be alone, without an ally in the world but Zero.

No entries to make in the Campaign, even, he thought.

There was only one thing left to do. He delved to the bottom of the pile and read back numbers till he heard the car return, when he hastily stuffed them back in position and went down. Zero he left behind.

Every dog has its day, he thought, and Zero's, it seemed, had already come and gone.

Chapter Eleven

SURPRISINGLY, JACK MANAGED to pull in a couple of unexpectedly good Mysterious Impressions that same evening. He had been determined on creating at least one, because he felt he should not let the sun go down on a totally non-productive day. If anything, it had been up to that point counter-productive.

After tea Grandma had gone to her room to breathe and asked Jack if he could bring along some incense sticks. He went up, tapped and entered. At first sight Grandma's room did not look like a bedroom so much as a photographic studio. The walls and all possible surfaces were crowded with portraits and snapshots. There were pictures of Grandma and Grandpa on their wedding day, both looking distinctly apprehensive, Jack thought, of Mr and Mrs Bagthorpe Junior on their wedding day, and of all the young Bagthorpes as babies. What there was most of, though, was Thomas. Thomas seated on Grandma's lap, her shoulders and feet. Thomas up trees, curtains and drainpipes. Thomas washing his ears, tail and toes, and Thomas, most of all, glowering, and looking toothy in a way that other cats never look toothy.

Grandma was sitting in an upright chair with a large old brass compass of Grandpa's on her lap.

"This is to line me up with the magnetic poles," she explained, seeing his surprised look. "That sort of detail is important."

She sounded like J. E. Fern of MYSTERIES. Next thing, she would probably find out about the electromagnetic fields of the earth as well, and start going round barefoot. She had selected two amber incense sticks and put one on each side of the dressing-table nearby. Jack lit them as Grandma composed herself in her chair.

"I'm quite excited," she told him. "You never know what might happen."

She closed her eyes, and began to inhale and exhale very slowly and very noisily. It was like Zero snuffing, only in very slow motion. The thin spirals of smoke began to drift towards her in the slight draught from the window.

"Aaaaah!" She let out a long, rapturous sigh.

Jack was rather disappointed in Grandma. He honestly thought she was too old for this kind of thing. He knew and accepted that his grandma would never be wise and calm like other people's, but he had never thought she would go to these lengths. He stared at the reflection of the incense. The dressing-table had a triple mirror and so it looked as if Grandma were wreathed in incense, as she had been in the smoke from her doomed birthday candles. Watching the slow whirl and spiral behind her he could see how easy it would be to go off into a trance if you kept watching long enough.

"What if I go off into a trance and can't come out of it!" came Grandma's alarmed voice.

It was as if she were voicing his own thoughts. Jack, still watching the threefold spiralling of the incense behind her left ear, did not reply, thinking she was speaking to herself, or at any rate that the question was merely rhetorical. Nor did it occur to him that she would have opened her eyes, since it was hardly two minutes since she had shut them.

There came a high, piercing scream. Grandma had shot right out of her chair and was staring into the dressing-table mirrors. Her own distraught face was in there now, veiled in the swirling incense.

"What is it?" she shrieked. "What do you see?"

Now Jack had not meant to do an MI on Grandma. But as she was already in as much of a lather as if he really had, there seemed no point in wasting an opportunity. Even if he said he had seen nothing, she wouldn't have believed him.

"I saw – swirling, like clouds drifting," he said slowly and to some extent truthfully, still staring into the mirror. Then, embroidering, "It is as if the heavens were opening!"

"Ooooooh," moaned Grandma. Then, "You don't see any faces. Tell me you can't see any faces!"

Jack shook his head.

"No faces," he told her. "Definitely. I've never seen a face – not yet."

"Nor a hooded figure?"

Jack shook his head again.

There was a tap on the door and William poked his head in. Grandma sat down again suddenly.

"Anything up, Grandma?" he asked. Then, "Poo – that horrible smell!"

"I think we had better put them out," Grandma told Jack. "You can take them back. I've changed my mind."

"I'm not surprised," William said. "Who was that screaming just then?"

"I heard no screaming," replied Grandma without batting an eyelid. "Perhaps you imagined it?"

Jack was astonished. It is an unusual thing to catch one's own Grandma out telling a fib.

"I don't imagine things," said William. "There's something rum up."

He sounded just like Mr Bagthorpe. Jack was annoyed by his inquisitorial manner.

"It could have been a disembodied voice," he suggested. "Funny we didn't hear it." (He decided that as Grandma had fibbed it was not only OK for him to do so too, but more or less his duty to back her up.) A flicker of uneasiness did momentarily pass over William's face.

"After all, there are such things." Jack pressed his point home. "You spend half your time listening to disembodied voices."

"Disembodied my foot," said William. "It's radio. It's different."

"I don't think it is," Jack said. "I think it's exactly the same. You never *see* any of these people, you only hear their voices. So how do you know they're real?"

"They – they've got numbers," William said. "They're in a book – you can look them up."

"Not Anonymous from Grimsby, you can't." Jack felt he had him now. "Funny the way *he* hasn't got a number and you can't look him up in the book."

"He's a pirate," said William.

"Or a disembodied voice," said Jack.

"Go away!" Grandma stood up again and flapped her hands at them. "Go away, both of you! I don't want to hear any of it. And tell Rosie I want her!"

"Sorry, Grandma," Jack said as he took his incense sticks. "I didn't really see anything much."

In the corridor outside Jack said thoughtfully:

"Funny the way that Anonymous from Grimsby is always talking about Intelligences in Outer Space."

"What d'you mean, funny?" demanded William.

"I mean – funny," said Jack, in what he hoped was an ominous tone.

"Go away, I said!" came Grandma's voice from behind the door. "I can still hear you!"

Jack went back along to his room and shut the door.

The second MI was also accidental. Jack found his eyes being constantly drawn to the box labelled CRYSTAL BALL FIRST QUALITY. Uncle Parker had had to pay a hefty deposit on it, and in a way it was probably the best prop Jack had. It would be a pity for it to have to go back to MYSTERIES without having had an airing. Jack admitted to himself that he did not much want to stare into it all on his own in his room, particularly in the evening. On the other hand, nor did he feel like taking it downstairs and planting it in the middle of a table and giving a public performance with it. He had not had any practice at this. There were all kinds of other arguments against this too, not least among them the possibility that Mr Bagthorpe would seize it and hurl it into the fireplace or somewhere, so costing Uncle Parker his deposit and Jack up to a year's pocket money.

He decided on a compromise. He thought that if he were out of doors he would probably be able to bring himself to stare into it. He did not know why it would feel safer to gaze out of doors, but he was sure it would.

I'll take Zero, he thought. *Then if he stiffens and his hairs stand on end and he starts off howling, I'll know to pack it in.*

Accordingly he sneaked out with Zero at his heels and took the box into the shrubbery beyond the back lawn. He took it only *just* inside the shrubbery, and not too far from the house. He remembered J. E. Fern's sepulchral warnings about "dabbling".

"I promise I'm not dabbling," he said out loud as he squatted behind a rhododendron and gently lifted the crystal ball from its box. He hoped whatever was in the ball had heard him. He repeated the words. "I'm definitely not dabbling," he said. "I'm dead serious."

The crystal ball looked very fragile and unearthly lying on the leaf-strewn ground by a laurel, with the lowering rays of the sun striking off it. Jack's knees were beginning to wobble so he changed from a crouching to a sitting position. (He had been crouching in much the way runners do in a race, poised to get off to a good start.)

"Lie, Zero!" he commanded. Zero lay immediately. He had been on the point of doing so anyway.

Jack was not certain exactly what procedure to adopt. He did not know how long he was supposed to gaze into the ball, whether he was supposed to make his mind go blank, and whether he should actually cup the ball in his hands. He decided against the last. He had vague recollections of seeing pictures of people gazing into crystal balls and they were usually on a table, a round one, and covered with a green velour cloth. The people looking into them had never, so far as he could remember, been children, which was a relief. Nine times out of ten they were female and swarthy and wore fringed shawls over their heads.

"They're definitely on tables," he decided, "not in people's hands."

He felt sure that if anything did appear in the crystal ball he would drop it, and run. He sat cross-legged, because it seemed more respectful and businesslike than sitting just anyhow, and began to gaze steadily into the crystal ball, only a couple of feet away on the ground.

He was very conscientious about keeping his gaze fixed absolutely non-stop on the ball because he knew this was essential if it were to have a chance to work. He began to feel rather queer once or twice, but he persisted. For a second he thought something was coming but then he blinked and it was gone.

"What you doin', Zack?" enquired a high voice right by his ear.

He jumped nearly out of his skin. If he had been holding the ball, he would certainly have dropped it. The reason why the voice had been right by his ear was that it belonged to Daisy Parker who was only about three and a half feet high.

"What's that?" she pointed. "I want to play with that pretty ball."

She went forward with the intention of picking it up, but Jack grabbed her.

"No!" he cried. Then, carefully, "No, Daisy. You see, the ball is magic."

"Mazic?" Her eyes widened. "Has it got a deathray?"

"Well, no," he told her. "At least, I can't say for sure. You never know."

Daisy edged backwards.

"Dai-sy! Dai-sy!" They were the high, trailing tones of Aunt Celia.

Jack groaned. In the distance he could hear other voices too.

"Mummy, Mummy, come quick!" Daisy pushed aside the rhododendron. "Come and look! Zack's got a mazic ball!"

Jack sat back and waited for the inevitable.

"I was playing hide-and-seek from you and I found Zack and Zero and a mazic ball!" Daisy was burbling. Now it was Jack's turn to feel like taking a piece out of her leg.

He looked up to see the tall swaying figure of Aunt Celia. Her eyes were riveted alarmingly on the crystal ball. Jack actually took another quick look into it himself, so sure was he that she was seeing something.

"Oooooh, oooooh," she moaned. "I see… oh…"

"What the devil's going on?" demanded Mr Bagthorpe's voice. "Get that fire-raising child out from among my shrubs."

"Come on, you lot!" It was William's voice. "Jack's having a Vision!"

When Jack next looked up there were four or five pairs of eyes peering round the rhododendron. There he sat with his crystal ball under a laurel, in broad daylight. It was ludicrous, even he could see that. If he had possessed the power to sink into the ground, even if never to return, he would have used it.

"I was practising," he said defensively. "You have to practise."

He noticed that Uncle Parker was walking away, supporting the leaning figure of his wife. Daisy had stopped to see the fun. Someone might get struck by a deathray.

"Jack, darling!" His mother pushed her way so hastily past the others that for one awful moment he thought she was going to overshoot and kick the crystal ball. He shut his eyes.

"Gypsy Petulengro, I believe?" said William in his sardonic voice. He was in a bad mood because Atlanta had not wanted to see the castle when she got to Aysham, and had gone off on her own, shopping instead. He was also still sore about Jack's insinuations about his Anonymous from Grimsby.

"Tell us, O Seer, what do you see?" he went on.

Right! Jack thought.

The situation could not possibly be worse, so he might as well turn it to the best use he could. If you do get caught looking into a crystal ball in such circumstances, at least you look less silly if you are actually seeing things in it. He fixed his eyes on the ball. A hush fell. He could hear his mother breathing heavily above him. Her Yoga always seemed to let her down when she most needed it.

"I see… I see…" He found the tone of his voice changing as he spoke, and actually felt a tingling in the nape of his neck. He really *did* think he saw…

"I see… I see… a sky… cloud… a Sign from above…"

Not a twig snapped in the Bagthorpe shrubbery. You could have heard a match strike.

"I see… a Giant Bubble, Bearing Tidings…" His voice trailed off. *Damn*, he thought, *I've gone and got it mixed up with Vision One*. As it happened, it was an inspired mistake.

"Golly," came Rosie's awed voice. "He was right about the Lavender Man. And now a Giant Bubble's going to Bear Tidings. Oh, Mummy, I'm scared."

Rosie was already rattled following her summons to Grandma's room. Grandma had absolutely forbidden her to put incense in the Portrait.

"Put Thomas in," she said, "lying in my lap, the way he used to. Those days will never come again."

Rosie had objected that she could not even remember Thomas because she had been only three when he was run over. All she could remember was once having some long, painful scratches on her arm which she had later been told Thomas had done when she had accidentally interrupted him washing his ears.

Grandma had insisted. The only thing left that could comfort her now, she said, was to have Thomas lying in her lap. And if she could not have it in real life, then at least she could have it in her Portrait. She had then started pulling down all the photographs of Thomas and thrust them into Rosie's arms.

"Take these," she said. "And remember, he was the most beautiful golden shining animal that ever lived. And his eyes! Never mind about my eyes and nose, but get his right."

With this poor Rosie had been bundled out of the room fruitlessly protesting that she couldn't draw cats anyway. She had gone back to her Portrait and had just been trying to paint out the incense sticks she had just painted in, when the Parkers arrived. This had given her an excuse to leave the Portrait, which she was beginning to hate the sight of. She was even beginning to feel that it had been her first Birthday Portrait that had triggered off all the terrible events of the last day or two.

Given all this, it was not, then, good news to Rosie to hear that a Giant Bubble Bearing Tidings was about to float on to the Bagthorpe horizon.

"I really am scared," she repeated.

"It may not come," comforted Mrs Bagthorpe, though without conviction. The Lavender Man had come.

"If it does, I'm not putting it in Grandma's Portrait!" Rosie was staring at the crystal ball.

"I'm not, I'm not! She's making me put Thomas in now, and I never even saw him!"

"There there!" said her mother weakly and led her out of the shrubbery. Only Daisy lingered.

"Is it still there?" she asked.

"What? Oh, no. It's gone."

Jack rose, his knees stiff, and stowed the ball back amongst its shavings in the box.

"CRYSTAL BALL FIRST QUALITY" she read out. It really was ridiculous the way she could read for a four-year-old. "What does that mean, Zack?" (One consolation was that half she read, she could not understand.)

"You're too young to understand. Come on, Zero."

As he passed the sitting-room on the way up to his room he could hear raised voices (raised, that is, even by Bagthorpian standards).

"–undermining this whole household," he heard his father shout. "And there's that dog at the bottom of it, and the fire-crazy daughter of yours! Where is she now? Where is she?"

"Out there," came Uncle Parker's voice.

"Well, get her out of out there! Get her in view, and don't let her out of it!"

Jack moved quietly off. He had heard what sounded very like matches rattling in a box when Daisy had moved out there in the shrubbery. If there was going to be another fire, at least he could make sure that Zero had an alibi.

As he passed Tess's room he could hear Atlanta's voice pronouncing English words slowly and carefully one after another. He gave a sharp rap on the door and shouted:

"Night! Just off to my room!" – to make sure his alibi could be properly authenticated.

The first thing he saw on entering his room was an envelope lying on his bed. It said JACK. PRIVATE on it in what was obviously disguised writing but was definitely Uncle Parker's disguised writing. He opened it.

"Why can't you keep that hound of yours in hand?" he read. "Don't let me catch him chewing anything of mine. I hear you got the Giant Bubble in. Good work. See you tomorrow 6.30 at same place, for further instructions."

It's all right for him, Jack thought. *It's not him that has to do it all. And I wish he wouldn't call Zero a hound.*

He took out his Plan of Campaign and began to make notes on the two latest MIs while they were clear in his mind. His mind was not staying clear for very long intervals these days. He was beginning to get confused about things.

After reporting the incense incident in Grandma's room Jack added with satisfaction:

"Got William rattled about Anon from Grimsby." (He did not know about Rosie's being rattled, or he would have put that in as well.)

He toned down the description of what happened in

the shrubbery, avoiding any mention of how silly he had felt, and doubtless looked, when discovered. He simply recorded the effect he had made on other people, which had been gratifying. He then put the book back in the middle of the pile of comics.

"Guard, Zero," he said. "Good boy."

Zero's tail twitched ever so slightly.

"Don't you worry, old chap," Jack told him. "We haven't finished yet. You're going to be the chosen dog of a Prophet."

Zero looked soulfully up at him from under his sprouting eyebrows. Jack gave him a thorough patting and praising, then got into bed. It wasn't really bedtime, but it had seemed a long-enough day.

Just before falling asleep he remembered something. He climbed out of bed, got a chair, and removed the box containing the crystal ball from the top of the wardrobe where he had put it for safekeeping. He did not know whether crystal balls invited Manifestations, but if they did, he preferred them to occur *inside* the wardrobe, out of his sight.

As he scrambled back into bed he remembered the early morning rendezvous. He set the alarm for six o'clock, and called it a day.

Chapter Twelve

JACK WAS WOKEN by the ringing of his alarm. He reached out to stop the bell and noticed that it had not affected Zero.

He's sinking into himself, he thought. *All he wants to do is sleep, to blot out the miseries of his existence.*

Once dressed he took out the Plan of Campaign so that he would not have to rely on his memory for the new instructions he was to receive. His memory had never been good, but he felt it was getting worse. He then roused Zero and quietly they padded out of the house.

He was right at the bottom of the garden when he saw to his astonishment a solitary figure sitting on the rustic seat overlooking the meadow. It was Grandpa. He was so still, and it was so amazing that he should be there at all, that Jack wondered if he had dropped off to sleep there the previous evening and had sat there all night, gathering dew. Jack edged carefully round to see him frontways on. His eyes were open all right – in fact they turned and rested on Jack himself.

"Hello, Grandpa!" he shouted.

"No need to shout," said Grandpa mildly. He turned his gaze away again over the meadow. "Just listening to the birds."

Listening to the birds*?* Jack thought. *So he* is *SD!*

If Grandpa could hear the dawn chorus but not Grandma, then that was the only possible explanation. It was as if his thoughts were being read.

"I can hear better first thing, before anybody's about," Grandpa said. "My hearing seems to get worse as the day goes on."

Jack nodded slowly. He could see what he meant. Bagthorpe days *were* long, trying affairs. His own faculties often felt bruised by the end of some of them.

"New aid's better, of course." Grandpa tapped it. "So far, so good. Have to see how the weather affects it."

"Yes," agreed Jack. "Anyway, I'm jolly glad, Grandpa. And the birds *do* sound smashing. I came out to listen to them myself partly. Going for a walk across to the wood."

He was still speaking loudly, from long habit, and pointed at the wood as he spoke, as if explaining to a young child, or Atlanta.

"Wish I'd got the legs to go with you," Grandpa told him. "Could've walked the legs off any of you when I was a boy."

"I bet you could," said Jack, though the notion of Grandpa ever having *been* a boy took him by surprise. "Bye, then. See you at breakfast."

"Get that dog of yours to catch a rabbit!" Grandpa shouted after him. Jack turned and waved.

"Hear that, Zero?" he said. "You're to catch a rabbit."

Once clear of the garden he broke into a jog to get himself into some kind of training for when he had to keep up with Uncle Parker. He was already fitter than he had been on the first rendezvous, because of all the hours of stick-fetching he had put in.

As he jogged along he thought again about Grandpa and how amazing it was that he should ever have been a boy, and gone rabbiting before breakfast. And following on this thought came the one that he, himself, might one day be somebody's grandpa and wear a hearing aid and get up early to listen to the dawn chorus. He then tried to imagine the others old – William, Tess and Rosie – and wondered where they would all be and what they would be doing.

And what with these thoughts and the golden brilliance of the morning and the satisfying rhythm he had now achieved, the whole business of not being a genius seemed to fall into place and become suddenly quite unimportant. He thought of his Campaign to become a Prophet and a Phenomenon, and actually laughed out loud.

"Me a Prophet!" he said to Zero. "And you the chosen dog of a Prophet!" – and laughed again.

This was not at all to say that he was going to abandon the whole scheme. On the contrary, it seemed more exciting than ever. He was enjoying it. All it really meant was that in that moment he abandoned any idea he might have had of ever *becoming* a Phenomenon or a genius. Playing the part of one for a time, and shaking up the others, was quite a different thing.

I've shaken them all up, he thought with satisfaction. *Even Mrs Fosdyke.*

He mentally went through the family and found that he had, indeed, shaken them all with the possible exception of Grandpa. Indirectly, he and Zero had done Grandpa a good turn. If his hearing aid had not been lost in Grandma's Birthday Fire he would not have been out sitting in the early sun and listening to the birds.

By now Jack was two fields away from home and out of sight. His timing had been perfect. There was Uncle

Parker now, rounding the copse and kicking up spray.

"Back to The Knoll!" he called, without stopping, and Jack fell in beside him.

"Did you know," asked Uncle Parker after a while, "that your father's shrubbery nearly went up last night?"

"Went up – you mean fire?"

"I mean Daisy," said Uncle Parker grimly. "Not content with losing a fistful of cracker mottoes and having a fire in her dolls' house. Broadening her activities."

"She really is what Father said she was, then. A pyro – whatever it was."

"Pyromaniac. Begins to look like it. Wasn't *born* one, I'm sure of it. It was that Birthday Party job that set her off. Keeps trying to recapture the excitement, I suppose. Natural enough."

"I suppose so," Jack agreed.

"Started a fire with some books at her playschool yesterday," went on Uncle Parker. "Luckily she was in the sandpit at the time. For heaven's sake don't tell your father."

"I won't," Jack promised.

"There is something you can do for me though. If ever Daisy comes round to your place with Celia and I'm not there – just give her a quick frisk for matches, will you?"

"Of course," Jack told him.

"Hasn't found out how to do it rubbing two sticks together yet," said Uncle Parker. "Though I suppose it's only a matter of time."

"She might grow out of it," Jack suggested. "It might be just a passing phase."

"Might be." He sounded dubious. "Let's hope we all live to find out. I've bought five fire extinguishers, anyway."

At The Knoll Uncle Parker went off to shower and change as before, and Jack sat and listened to the birds and gave Zero a pep talk.

"Never forget," he told him, "that it's your own opinion of yourself that matters, not other people's." Mrs Bagthorpe often told people this in her letters about their Problems.

Uncle Parker was carrying his own Plan of Campaign when he reappeared.

"Now!" he said briskly. "Big developments."

"Good," Jack said.

"We carry on with Prong One of the attack as usual. You know – the odd Mysterious Impression slipped in here and there as and when you see an opening."

"Right." Jack noted it down.

"Prong Two I'll come back to in a minute," Uncle Parker told him. "Start a fresh page, and head it Prong Three, and at the side of it write 'Dowsing'."

"Oh. We're starting that, are we?"

"You must diversify," Uncle Parker told him, "if you're going to keep that lot on their toes."

"Have several Strings to my Bow, you mean?" Jack had not thought he would live to see the day. He really was getting to be equal.

"You have already sown the seeds of doubt in their minds. You have seen things behind their ears, you have made a prophecy that was fulfilled, and you have also made a prophecy about a Giant Bubble."

"I wish I knew what all this about a Giant Bubble is," Jack said.

"You will, in time. Let's come back to Prong Three. You have to be seen to be a full-time Phenomenon. It is no use spending the odd few minutes a day having visions and then carrying on as normal the rest of the time. It doesn't convince. You have reached the stage of becoming a full-timer. When you are not seeing things past people's ears or looking into your crystal ball, you must be seen to be doing other, equally baffling things. Do you take my point?"

Jack said that he did.

"So this is it."

Uncle Parker reached under the stone bench and fetched out a forked hazel branch.

"Now watch me."

He took a fork in each hand and began to walk steadily forward with his palms turned upward and his gaze fixed steadily on the tip of the twig.

"This is how you must hold it. You'll find it all in the Manual, but it's easier to understand if you actually see it done. Here, you have a go."

Jack took the hazel and tried to position it as Uncle Parker had done, in his palms.

"That's the ticket. Keep it light. Don't grip it. There's a good chance, you know, you might really get to do it. Says in this book children up to the age of fourteen or so are often natural dowsers."

"Does it really?" Jack liked the feel of the hazel in his hands. It really did feel taut and sprung, as if ready to leap.

"And there's another thing. No harm my telling you. I've looked up one or two old maps and you've got a couple of underground watercourses right on your doorstep."

"In the garden?"

"Don't know about in the garden. But that big meadow at the bottom. Somewhere in there. So you're in luck. You'll make sure somebody actually *sees* you dowsing, and you're in with a chance of actually striking gold – water."

"Crikey." Jack was impressed. He could hardly wait to begin. He thought he could feel his palms tingling already.

"You can keep that stick," Uncle Parker told him. "Might even be better than the one you've got – you never know. Temperamental, these dowsing rods. And if you don't do anything with one, you can change to the other. It'll look to everyone as if it's the rod that's wrong, not you."

Jack could see that it would.

"Right. So that's Prong One and Prong Three dealt with. We're back to Prong Two."

"And the Giant Bubble."

"I'm still not going to tell all," Uncle Parker said. "It isn't politic. Not yet. But I want some more foundations laying. The first I shall do for myself. It's Rosie's birthday next week, right?"

"She'll be nine. Catching me up."

"Don't be an idiot," Uncle Parker told him. "How can she? What I shall do, is trot along to your place later on today, and say that I am going to provide a Birthday Party."

"Smashing."

"I shall go on to say, in light-hearted vein, that as Daisy is coming and we don't want to risk a conflagration, the party will take the form of a picnic, and will be held in the meadow."

"What if it rains?" Jack asked.

"If it rains, we'll have to make the best of a bad job and have it in the house. And at least if there's a fire the rain'll be useful. And I'll bring a couple of extinguishers," he added.

"What's the foundation I've got to lay?" Jack wanted to know.

"That's the question. Now look, if you were a man and didn't want to be recognised, what would you disguise yourself as? I mean, what disguise would you have that would be absolutely foolproof? No good just tacking on beards and moustaches. Too risky."

"Are you going to disguise *yourself*?"

"No, I'm not. It's a friend of mine."

Jack thought for a while.

"What about a bear?" he suggested at length.

"First class!" Uncle Parker clapped him on the shoulder. "Just the ticket – oh, what a – oh, I can hardly wait!"

"But how do I come into it?"

"How you come into it, Jack, old son, is that you now start trimming up your Vision a bit. Did you get the red and white in?"

"No," admitted Jack. "I tried, but there were too many people shouting and screaming."

"Well, get it in. Quick. Today. And once that's sunk in, then go on to the Great Brown Bear bit. Yes, that sounds good – I see… I see… it is the Age of the Bear, the Great Brown Bear…"

Jack was rapidly making notes.

"Don't overdo it with your father," Uncle Parker told him. "The strain's beginning to tell. You can let him see you dowsing, but steer clear of him with the Bear."

"Right. That all?"

"For now. And for goodness' sake don't lose that book. It's red hot now, with all that stuff in. Pity we didn't think of using a code."

"You needn't worry," Jack told him, "it's in the safest place in the whole house. It's in among my comics. No one in our house would be caught dead looking at them."

"That's true." Uncle Parker had been present on some of the occasions when the Bagthorpian views on Rubbishy Reading were being aired. "Good thinking, Jack."

"Besides, Zero's guarding them most of the time," Jack said. Uncle Parker made no comment on this. He changed the subject.

"How's Atlanta going on, by the way?"

"All right. She's a bit of a bind.You have to keep repeating things and pointing all the time."

"Ah." Uncle Parker looked relieved. "She can't speak English, then. I wasn't too sure why she didn't say anything while I was driving her over."

"I think William's gone on her," Jack told him. "He wants to take up Danish for his sixth String to his Bow, but Tess won't let him. They keep having rows about it."

"Bit of a fly in the ointment, that girl," said Uncle Parker, half to himself. "Whichever way you look at it."

"What d'you mean?"

"Oh. Oh, nothing. We've already solved that one, anyway."

"Solved what?" Jack was mystified.

"Off you go, now." Uncle Parker stood up. "Better get back before Daisy's up and rooting round for matches. If I can keep her from starting a fire for a few days on the trot, it might break the habit."

He hurried off, stooping where necessary under the arched roses, definitely keyed up by Daisy's alarming new propensity. It could hardly be doing Aunt Celia any good either, Jack reflected. He felt sorry for Uncle Parker, having to live with two such problems. It seemed to Jack that he deserved better. On the other hand, no one knew better than himself that families are really something that just happen to you, nothing to do with choice.

He broke into a run.

"Come on, Zero, old chap. I'll be able to pull in a fry-up before Fozzy gets in, if we hurry. At the double!"

Chapter Thirteen

JACK PULLED IN his fry-up and the day seemed off to a good start, as so often the really bad days do.

The Bagthorpe family were bad-tempered and edgy and they were all boasting more than usual. This was a sign that they were feeling threatened. It was not merely that Jack's totally unexpected and rather alarming new talents looked like overshadowing them all. It was just a general sense that after the last few days anything could happen, and if it did, it would almost certainly be bad.

Grandma evidently had this feeling so strongly that she was keeping to her room again. She said she felt safer in there. She was obviously not spending the whole time breathing, because she kept sending communiqués to

Rosie asking her to hurry up with the Portrait so that she could have her photographs of Thomas back.

This, in turn, made Rosie feel threatened. She was tempted to make such a horrible mess of the painting that she would lose her reputation for doing portraits and never have to do one again. She decided against this in the end. She liked doing portraits usually, and if she never did any more she would have lost a String to her Bow and have to find another one. So she struggled on. She gave Grandma a nose, eyes and mouth this time, and in fact put in a lot more detail than she had intended, to defer the evil moment when she would have to tackle Thomas. Only when she had added the last possible wrinkle to Grandma's brow did she face up to the inevitable. She glared at the pictures of Thomas spread before her and thought how ugly and bad-tempered he looked and could understand why everyone had hated him so much alive. He was hateful dead, as far as Rosie was concerned.

Downstairs William and Tess were battling for Atlanta's attention. The former was showing her the silver cups and trophies he had won for tennis. He had first taken them into the kitchen with a request that Mrs Fosdyke should clean them. This, in turn, had put Mrs Fosdyke into a bad temper.

"I've no time for that kind of fiddle-faddling today," she told him. "Mrs Bagthorpe and me've got the decorators coming in. We've carpets to choose and curtains to choose and lord knows what else though I'm bound to say that room'll never be what it was. Hairlooms, them chairs was, and even if you could get 'em the same again identical, they wouldn't be the same."

William had cleaned the silver himself, the more to impress Atlanta. He was definitely gone on her. And not only that, word seemed to have gone round, because some of Jack's friends, and their elder brothers as well, had started turning up at the house on all sorts of pretexts.

This, in turn, was annoying Mr Bagthorpe. After breakfast he had retired to his study to try out the new microphone, though with little hope of success.

"I might've yesterday. I was on the brink of a breakthrough when that hellhound came pouncing down on me. I can't sit saying my thoughts out loud. It's not in my nature. I'm too shy. It makes me self-conscious."

The others were so stunned by Mr Bagthorpe's claim to shyness that they could think of nothing to say.

"I know what you'll do," he went on. "You'll creep up outside my door and listen, I know you will."

They all strenuously denied this. The thought had not even entered their heads, they said, though one or two of them did make a mental note that it would be quite an interesting thing to do to fill in the odd spare moment.

When William's friends started turning up, however, and started playing music and laughing loudly, Mr Bagthorpe came out of his room and shouted:

"What is this? A commune? Turn that thing off! I'll never write another word. I'm finished."

He gave a despairing wave of his white arm and went back in and banged the door, and there was some muffled shouting in there for a time, which was presumably Mr Bagthorpe doing some strong dialogue. Then silence.

William told his friends they had better go, and they reluctantly went, still staring at Atlanta. William fetched a spare racket and took her out on to the lawn to coach her tennis. Tess, infuriated by this, brought out a mat and began practising all kinds of Judo falls and at the same time talking to Atlanta and pointing things out to her and maddening William. The Bagthorpes were never at their best when out to impress, and once one of them started showing off, they usually went right out of control. It was infectious. Rosie, sitting alone in her room with the Birthday Portrait, stuffed the photos of Thomas into her folio and went out to set her things up in the garden too.

Atlanta was gratifyingly impressed. She went through all the paintings in Rosie's folio and exclaimed "Bootiful", or "Vot Gut", at everything, and Rosie was so flattered that she offered to paint Atlanta's portrait when she had finished Grandma's.

"Oh *ja ja*, plees plees!" Atlanta was delighted. William was not. On the other hand, it gave him an idea, and he went and fetched his camera and finished the film in it taking shots of Atlanta.

By then Rosie had set up her easel and restarted work on the Birthday Portrait. Atlanta came and looked over her shoulder. She frowned a little. She pointed to the row of photos of Thomas that Rosie had clipped along the top of the easel, and then at the indeterminate gingery shape Rosie had so far roughed in on Grandma's lap.

"Cat," said Rosie, and pointed to Thomas up a drainpipe with a mouse in his mouth.

"Cat," repeated Atlanta. Then, pointing to the ginger blur, repeated in mystified tones, "*Cat?*"

"I can't do cats," said Rosie glumly. "Meant to be one. But I can't do cats." She shook her head vigorously to convey this. Atlanta's face instantly lit up.

"Ah! Me – me – I do cats. Plees?"

She put out her hand for the brush and Rosie, a trifle dazed, gave it to her. Atlanta moved into position before the easel. It was at this point that Jack came out, armed with the two dowsing rods and followed by Zero. He had hoped to attract some attention, but was not even registered as present. Tess, William and Rosie were all watching with rapt admiration as Atlanta painted with swift, deft strokes. Intrigued, Jack went over and joined them. He had to join them anyway, if he wanted them to notice his dowsing gear.

Rosie's impression of Grandma was in itself spectacular. The formerly missing eyes, nose and mouth were there all right, but so enmeshed in a network of lines and wrinkles that at first sight she looked more like an ordnance survey map than a person. But what was amazing, what riveted the eye, was the gingery bundle on her lap which was becoming, literally second by second, the living image of the late, ill-fated Thomas. Even Jack did not remember the original very well, but he had seen his photographs and heard enough stories about his character and exploits to recognise that this, to the life, was he.

No one spoke as Atlanta's brush darted back and forth. The Bagthorpes respected other people's Strings to Bows, and the likeness was in any case breathtaking, from narrowed eyes to unsheathed claws and stiffened tail. At length Atlanta stepped back from the easel and half closed her eyes and murmured:

"*Ja?*"

"Oh *ja*!" chorused the Bagthorpes as one. Rosie rushed

forward and actually hugged Atlanta. The portrait, the dreadful Birthday Portrait, was finished, and what was more, Grandma was going to like it.

Grandma not only liked it, she actually wept before it. She said it was as if Thomas had stepped out of time and was there with her again, breathing and purring as ever was. (No one else remembered Thomas doing much purring, but perhaps she did.) She said that she would never be parted from the portrait as long as she lived, and the Bagthorpes half expected her to announce her intention of having it buried with her.

Now, however, while the Bagthorpes were congratulating Atlanta, and Tess was doing some complicated falls to try to draw attention, Jack himself had a sudden inspiration.

She's captured that cat, he thought, *even from the grave. What if she could capture Zero? O Zero, old chap – the thought stunned him – you'd be immortal!*

He wasted no time. He stepped forward, tapped Atlanta's arm, and pointed at Zero with one of the divining rods.

"Dog," he said.

"Dorg," agreed Atlanta. "Sero."

"That's right. You – you *paint* dorg?" he pointed first at the still wet paint on Thomas, and then at Zero. Her face lightened.

"*Ja, ja*. I do dorg. I do Sero."

"Oh, *please*," Jack said. "Will you?"

She nodded.

"I like to. I like do Sero. Rosie?" She pointed at the easel and paints. Rosie could not at that moment have refused her anything.

"Now?" Jack felt it best to act while the time was ripe.

"*Ja. Ja.*"

William, disgusted, threw down his racket.

"I'm off," he said. "I'm going to have a word with Anonymous from Grimsby." He went.

There was a confused period then in which it was established, after much repetition and pointing, that Atlanta would gladly undertake Zero's portrait, but did not feel up to Jack's. It was arranged that she should paint Zero, here and now, and that Rosie, who was, after all, the acknowledged portrait painter, should fill Jack in later.

And this is what happened. Jack put down his rods and sat on the grass with Zero beside him. Tess and Rosie watched, fascinated, as Atlanta clipped up her paper and set to work. Jack himself could not see how the portrait was going but could tell from the expression on the others' faces that Zero's was at least as good as, if not better than, Thomas's. He was enchanted by this entirely unexpected development. Nothing in the world, it seemed to him, would boost Zero's confidence more than to see a faithful portrait of himself hung in a place of honour in the Bagthorpe residence. Having your portrait painted was a sign that you have arrived, he thought, and wished that he could write poetry so that he could do a fitting epitaph for Zero as Byron had for his dog Boatswain.

Not that he's dead yet, he thought, and pushed the thought away because it was one he could not bear to contemplate. He took a sideways look at Zero to see what kind of an angle his ears were set at, but could not really judge from profile.

Mrs Bagthorpe appeared, followed by Mrs Fosdyke. They both exclaimed extravagantly on the portrait of Grandma and Thomas which was lying in the sun to dry before being taken up and presented.

"That's terribly good of Grandma, Rosie," Mrs Bagthorpe told her. (She would have said this however true or untrue it was. She believed strongly in the power of praise.)

"It's the spitting image of that horrible cat of hers," observed Mrs Fosdyke. "Gives you the creeps to look at it. He looks just like he's sizing up to take a spring at you." This was something Thomas had done a lot of, and one of the things that had made him so universally feared and hated.

"Oh – and look at this!" Mrs Bagthorpe was now peering over Atlanta's shoulder. "Oh, it's beautiful, Atlanta."

William, who had evidently not managed to make contact with Anonymous from Grimsby, now reappeared. He was carrying the darts and board, which he intended to set up in the summer house and then invite Atlanta to have a game. Playing darts was by way of being a very minor fifth String to William's Bow.

"She's never painting that object," he said. Then, grudgingly, "It looks like him."

Jack could bear the suspense no longer.

"Stay, Zero," he commanded, and went round behind the easel.

Zero had, no doubt about it, been captured, from his round black nose to his great furry paws. Even the colour was exactly right, pale honey shading through to tips of auburn on his tail. Jack actually felt a lump in his throat.

"Looks that real you could give him a bone," was Mrs Fosdyke's judgement, and Jack thought it very handsome of her, even if Atlanta could not understand the compliment.

"*Ja?*" Again Atlanta stepped back to survey her work and again the Bagthorpes chorused an enthusiastic "*Ja*!"

"Shall we let him dry before you do me?" Jack asked Rosie. "We don't want to risk smudging him. In any case, there's something I want to do. I feel as if I'm being drawn to it by an invisible magnet."

He picked up the divining rods.

"You're barmy," said William. "They're divining rods, they are."

"I know," said Jack.

"You can't divine," William told him.

"I wouldn't be so sure," said Jack in what he hoped were mysterious tones.

"Oh dear." Mrs Bagthorpe was looking worried again by this new evidence of her son's eccentricity. "Do be careful, Jack."

"I will," he promised. "Come on, Zero."

He walked off down towards the wicket gate feeling the gaze of the others following him. Once in the meadow he decided to give the rod from MYSTERIES first try. He fitted the forks into the palms of his hands as Uncle Parker had shown him, and set off, Zero at his side.

It was not easy, he soon discovered, to walk in long grass over uneven ground and keep your eyes fixed unwaveringly on a point only a couple of feet under your nose. Twice he stumbled in rabbit holes and fell. Matters were not helped by Zero, who evidently thought that this was going to develop at any moment into a new form of the stick-fetching game, and kept prancing excitedly about and getting in the way. Twice Jack found himself about to walk right into a tree.

I'll never know whether I've covered the whole ground, he thought, *because I can't see where I'm going. I'm like a thirsty traveller lost in the desert and going round and round in circles looking for an oasis.*

The only way round this that he could see would be to fill his pockets with dried peas or rice or something as Hansel and Gretel did, and he thought he would probably have to end up doing this. The sun baked down and Jack found it easy to maintain the illusion of being in a desert. He seemed to be walking for a very long time and his arms were beginning to ache. He had the feeling that no one was even watching him, and that he might be wasting his time. Once or twice he did think he felt the stick quiver but when he stopped to test this, he realised it was only because his arms were tired and beginning to tremble.

I can't keep it up much longer, he thought.

As it happened he didn't. The thought was barely out of his head when his foot caught in something. The rod flew out of his hand and he fell headlong. There was an almighty yell. Zero was barking madly and had his nose down and Jack glimpsed a long length of black flex. History was repeating itself.

Jack grabbed at it. It was too late. Zero had it in his mouth and was off. Jack scrambled to his feet and set off after him. Behind him he could hear his father's yells.

"Get him! Get the brute before he chews it up again!"

This time Jack did catch Zero before he got to the mike-chewing stage. He had just settled by the hedge with it between his paws when Jack caught up. He whipped away the flex and saw to his relief that the microphone was intact. Mr Bagthorpe was approaching, breathless, his red face contrasting arrestingly with his white arm. He was not, strangely enough, shouting. He seemed to be past shouting.

"Tell me," he said. "Go on – tell me."

"No – it's all right – look!" Jack held out the flex and Mr Bagthorpe examined the microphone.

"It'll be broken inside," he said. "It's been rattled all over this field. It'll be broken inside."

"I don't think it will," Jack told him. "And even if it is, it won't be Zero's fault this time, it'll be mine."

"What got into you?" asked Mr Bagthorpe, as if he really wanted to know. "What have I ever done to you that you should walk deliberately on to me and my work? And why have you been half the morning walking round this field like a sleepwalker with a twig in your hand?

You know, don't you, that whatever that numbskulled doctor thinks, I think you need some kind of treatment?"

"Yes, I know," said Jack. "And I know it must've looked funny to an outsider the way I was walking round."

"Funny?" said Mr Bagthorpe. "Funny is right. You don't by any chance feel that you might be Moses?"

"No," Jack told him. "I'm dowsing. Water divining."

"I see." Mr Bagthorpe sounded really world-weary now. "He's divining. Well, of course that explains everything, I suppose. Where the devil did I leave the other half of this?" He waved the microphone.

"I'll help you look," Jack said. "And Zero. Find, Zero!"

Zero did not understand this instruction but the way Jack said it sounded exciting, so he acted as if he did and began prancing about and snuffing.

"Stop him!" yelled Mr Bagthorpe, galvanised again. "I don't want him finding it. *I'll* find it."

Jack called Zero and they all walked along looking about them as they went. It was not going to be easy to find a portable recorder in grass that long.

"I thought you were doing it in your study," Jack said. "I wasn't expecting to fall over you."

"I told you," said Mr Bagthorpe. "There are listening ears. I've got to have privacy. If you're a creative writer you need privacy like a cow needs a salt lick."

"I'm sure nobody was listening," Jack said. "We were all too busy."

"I may as well tell you –" Mr Bagthorpe sounded pleased despite himself – "that I have, despite having you go round me in circles all morning with that wand, I have done some work. Quite a lot, in fact."

"Oh good, I'm really glad."

"I've done some of the best work I've ever done. And all my thoughts are in that recorder somewhere in this grass, and that's why it's got to be found," said Mr Bagthorpe. "It's my last link with sanity."

In the end it was Jack who spotted it.

"There!" he cried, and pointed.

"Keep that dog back," ordered Mr Bagthorpe. He advanced and picked up the recorder. He stood there looking at it and all at once Jack could see something was wrong. He watched for a long time as his father stared down.

"Oedipus had it made," said Mr Bagthorpe dully at last. "Lear was a lucky man. Don't tell me Hamlet had problems."

All the spirit seemed to have gone out of him. He began to lurch away in the direction of the house. Jack and Zero followed at a distance.

Mr Bagthorpe did not emerge from his study till the

evening. He said later that he had not trusted himself. What had evidently happened was that someone, somehow, had pressed the wrong buttons on the recorder and GREAT THOUGHTS: DO NOT ERASE had, irrevocably, been erased. It was clear that he laid the blame for this at the feet of Jack and Zero. Jack, while sorry it had happened, was not so sure. Mr Bagthorpe was notorious for breaking anything mechanical and had probably already pressed the wrong buttons when Jack fell on top of him. He had probably been pressing wrong buttons all morning and his GREAT THOUGHTS: DO NOT ERASE had not even been recorded in the first place. A man who can break a toaster, a record player and a waste disposal in a single week (Mr Bagthorpe's all-time record so far) is obviously the kind of man who presses wrong knobs.

Mr Bagthorpe's brooding presence behind the closed door of the study cast something of a blight over the rest of the household and Jack wished he did not have to do what he still had to do, which would upset everybody still more. But he had a Plan of Campaign, and he had to stick to it.

In the afternoon Rosie said that she wanted to do Jack's portrait. She had received so much praise for Grandma's that she was greedy for more. She suggested that the burnt-out dining-room would be a good background for this portrait too, because it would throw Zero's honey coat into relief. Jack agreed. He squatted on the blackened carpet, which was at least dry by now.

At first things went well enough. No one else was there and as the Bagthorpes tended only to say clever or sardonic things when there was an audience, conversation was normal enough. Jack suggested that Rosie should do a Self-Portrait for her own birthday the following week and she was delighted by this idea.

"What I can do," she said, "is to do a Birthday Self-Portrait every year as long as I live, and then I can hang them in rows and it'll be really interesting. I bet nobody's ever done that before in the whole history of painting. Thank you, Jack."

She was very happy, humming as she mixed her paints and making little remarks like:

"I think your face has got more interesting since you started having Visions and things. It was a bit blank before."

It was this particular remark that reminded Jack again of what he had to do before the day was out. He didn't want to do anything immediately because he didn't really want to make Rosie his victim if he could help it. He wondered who might be suitable. Grandma and Mr Bagthorpe were both out, and Atlanta too, on the grounds that the language barrier would prevent her from understanding what a Great Brown Bear was. William was not a good prospect because he would probably only sneer and not even bother to tell the rest of the family. He was still pondering when Tess came in.

"Seen Atlanta?" she asked. Rosie and Jack shook their heads.

Tess came up behind Rosie and started looking at Jack and then back to the portrait, assessing the likeness. Quick as thought, Jack fixed his gaze on the blackened wall just behind Tess's left ear. He could not of course, see what effect this was having, but he heard Tess whisper to Rosie:

"Look! Look at him. Is that how he looks?"

"Oh dear!" Rosie jumped up. "It is, it is!"

Another minute and they would both be out of the room.

"I see… I see…" Jack murmured. "A Giant Bubble. I see red… I see white… and clouds…"

"We've had this one before," he heard Tess whisper. "He's having the same Vision as yesterday."

"–and I see… Oh, it is the Age of the Bear. A Great Brown Bear…"

There were two squeals in close succession and Jack removed his gaze in time to catch sight of the rapidly retreating backs of Rosie and Tess.

That's done, he thought with satisfaction. *That'll soon be round the house.*

He was right. He had only just got up to inspect the portrait, which was, fortunately, practically finished, when Mrs Bagthorpe entered. She came straight to him and put her hand on his forehead more from force of habit than anything. She removed it almost immediately.

"It is a hot day, of course..." she murmured.

"What's up, Mother?" Jack enquired. "Like my portrait?"

"It's wonderful, darling. A speaking likeness. But oh Jack, what do you mean? What *kind* of a Great Brown Bear, and where?"

The memory of how quickly the Lavender Man had materialised after Jack's prediction was clearly still with her.

"Bear?" he repeated. "What bear?"

"Rosie and Tess are in a dreadful state," she told him.

"Oh. Have I had another Vision?" asked Jack.

"I'm afraid you have. And this time, you saw not only a Giant Bubble, but a Great Brown Bear, apparently."

She sounded so worried that she would have undoubtedly written a letter to Stella Bright for advice, had the thing been feasible.

Grandma was the next to arrive, and she wanted Jack to describe the bear, because she thought it might have been a vision of Thomas he had been having.

"He wasn't brown, of course, he was the most beautiful auburn and gold," she said. "But anyone not very colour-conscious might *think* he was brown."

Jack got out of this by saying he had no clear memory of what he had seen.

"I just have this hazy impression," he said, "and it definitely wasn't the right shape for a cat."

Grandma didn't give up straight away because she had already set her heart on a resurrection of Thomas. The whole of the rest of the day was given over to a thorough examination of Jack's latest Vision and what its meaning might be. It was as thorough a Bagthorpian Post-Mortem as there had ever been.

The thing was looked at from every conceivable angle and everyone had something to say. Grandma was sticking to her Thomas theory even after Jack had told her that vague as his impression was he was now sure it did not have whiskers. William was taken up with the red and white aspect of it, and concocting elaborate theories to do with Yorkshire and Lancashire, despite the fact that none of the Bagthorpes had ever been anywhere near either of these counties. Tess came up with the idea that there was to be an imminent return to an Ice Age, and that the red and white was people's blood on the snow once the Great Brown Bear got going. The Giant Bubble, she ingeniously explained, was an igloo. Rosie stuck her fingers in her ears while Tess was talking like this. All in all, Mrs Fosdyke was perhaps the most decisive in her reaction.

"The day a Great Brown Bear walks in this house," she said, "I walk out. You can call it Provisional Notice, if you like."

Jack went to the trouble of recording this in his Campaign Book that night.

We've got it in writing now, he thought.

Chapter Fourteen

JACK HAD GUESSED that something was amiss at The Knoll when Uncle Parker had not turned up later in the day to make his offer to Rosie of a Birthday Picnic. He had also guessed it was something to do with Daisy. Once or twice during the evening he had slipped out and stood at the bottom of the garden scanning the skyline for signs of smoke. He was not, however, sufficiently curious to set his alarm for 6 a.m. and go for yet another early morning jog. He decided to get quietly on with his own Prongs and await developments.

The following day got off to a fairly brisk start with Mr Bagthorpe summoning everyone to breakfast. He did this by walking about the house banging on doors and shouting:

"Up! Up, everyone! I want you all in the kitchen in five minutes flat!"

Everyone was there. Grandma need not have been, because there was no reason why she should obey her son's orders, especially when they were given in so noisy and rude a way. It was curiosity that brought her down.

"Now," said Mr Bagthorpe, when they were all assembled, "who's got fewest Strings to their Bow?"

"He has," said Tess, Rosie and William instantly, pointing to Jack.

"Not counting him," said Mr Bagthorpe. "Leave him out of it."

William ticked his off on his fingers, watching Atlanta out of the corner of his eye.

"Electronics, tennis, pure mathematics, drums, and you might say darts. Five."

"Tess?"

"French, oboe, piano, Judo and Danish coming up. Five."

"You can't count Danish," William objected. "If you do, I'm going to as well."

"Be quiet," Mr Bagthorpe told him. "Rosie?"

"Violin, maths, portraits and I think I'm going to have swimming as well."

"I wonder if you'd be any good at it," murmured Mr

Bagthorpe thoughtfully. "I wonder… Let's have a look at your hands."

Rosie, mystified, spread out her hands and everyone took a good look at them and wondered what they were supposed to be looking for.

"They might be big enough," decided Mr Bagthorpe. "We'll give it a try. Report to me in my study at nine."

"What for?"

Mr Bagthorpe now started on his breakfast, the business side of things having been dealt with. He took a slice of toast and pushed it towards Tess.

"Butter this, please," he said, "and plenty of marmalade. Yes. Well. Yesterday, alone in my study after my trauma in the meadow, I had time for thought."

"Every cloud has a silver lining, you see, dear," said his wife. "Normally, you *never* have time for thought."

He shot her a hard look and continued.

"I have decided to persevere with the use of that infernal recording machine, despite all attempts at sabotage."

"They weren't sabotage," Jack said. "They were accidents."

"I owe it to my public," Mr Bagthorpe said. "I owe it to the BBC. 'Thou shalt not hide your torch under a bush' and all that."

Mr Bagthorpe never normally quoted from the Bible, even inaccurately, and Mrs Bagthorpe looked at him as though she wondered if he could be slowly going the same way as Jack.

"When I have spoken my thoughts into the machine," he said, "they will have to be typed. I cannot type."

He waved the arm, which was not such a pure white now. It was showing signs of wear and tear.

"I need someone to type for me. Rosie can have a go."

"Oh, must I?" Rosie wailed. "I don't think I'll be able to. I think my hands are too little."

"We'll see," he said.

"And you'll shout at me if I make mistakes," she said. "You know you will."

Mr Bagthorpe did not reply to this. He clearly did not feel he could give any assurances about not shouting.

"If we're all going to be devoured at any moment by a Great Brown Bear," said William, "I don't see the point in your bothering with any more scripts."

"Oh, don't! Don't talk about it!" pleaded Rosie.

Jack kept his eyes on his plate.

"Calm yourself," Grandma told Rosie. "Jack *thinks* he saw a Great Brown Bear, but I am convinced that what he really saw was a Vision of Thomas."

"For crying out loud, Mother," said Mr Bagthorpe, "don't start on about that again. And even if you're right, I see no comfort in it. Personally, given the choice between a

Great Brown Bear and that malevolent ginger brute, I'd settle for the bear any day."

"I don't think you realise how hurt I am when you say things like that!" Grandma told him.

"I'm sorry, Mother," he said, "but it's the way I feel. If you're a creative writer, the one thing you must have is honesty. I've got to be honest, even when it hurts."

When Uncle Parker did turn up about an hour later, Rosie was closeted with her father in the study. There were a lot of uneven typing noises going on, and also the first signs that Mr Bagthorpe was going to begin shouting.

Uncle Parker told Mrs Bagthorpe of his plan for the following Wednesday, and she was delighted by it.

"How very kind, Russell," she said. "Rosie is in the study helping Henry. Go along there and you can tell her yourself."

Jack went and sat just inside the sitting-room opposite the study, and pretended to read a magazine. He knew that usually Mr Bagthorpe would not let Uncle Parker into his study. He said he upset the vibrations in there. He was very funny about whom he would or would not let go in there, and had once even stopped the vicar from doing so. He said that vibrations build up in a room, and if you are a sensitive creative writer, you have to have the right ones.

He must have really believed this because he would not let Mrs Fosdyke clean up in there and actually hoovered it himself about once a fortnight.

"Her vibrations," he declared, "would play havoc with a saint's. If she went in there, it'd take six months for the room to settle down again."

When Uncle Parker tapped on the door and entered, therefore, Jack knew there would be a reaction.

"Morning, Henry."

"Get back, get back!" Mr Bagthorpe had sure enough leapt forward and was barring the way with arms outspread.

"Sorry, old chap. I forgot. All that vibration stuff. You might be right, of course. All this business of Jack and his Visions, and so forth."

"Don't talk to me about Jack or his Visions," said Mr Bagthorpe coldly.

"All right. I came to have a word with Rosie, here, actually."

"Did you really?" Rosie, seeing her chance of escape, jumped up from the desk. "What about?"

He told her. Rosie was ecstatic.

"Oh, it'll be lovely," she told him. "Thank you."

"And there will be crackers," he assured her, less than altruistically. "Two each, to make up for last time."

"At least there's less likely to be a fire at this party,"

observed Mr Bagthorpe. "Though I wouldn't put any money on it."

Reactions to the suggestion varied. William said there were a lot of ants in the meadow and that the grass was seeding and would probably give him hay fever and he would rather have the party in the house.

"We have no dining-room, dear," Mrs Bagthorpe reminded him.

Grandma said it was a pity Rosie's birthday came so soon after her own because she did not feel she had completely recovered from that yet. She said she would come to the party if it was fine, and if not would watch it from an upper window through Grandpa's field glasses.

"I shall be able to capture the spirit of it," she said. "And I probably shan't be missed."

Mrs Fosdyke put in an unsuccessful protest.

"I know I'm not clever like you," she told the family, "but I don't see the point in carting food to be eaten in the middle of a field at the bottom of your garden. People that has picnics, usually goes in cars."

"There is a reason why it should be this particular field, Mrs Fosdyke," Uncle Parker assured her. "All will become clear on the eleventh."

"Why not the summer house?" she asked.

"Not big enough," said Jack quickly.

"Oh well." She shrugged and gave up. "One thing, it'll be paper cups and plates. There's none of my china going down that field, thank you very much."

Jack managed a few minutes alone with Uncle Parker on the pretext of showing him how Zero could fetch sticks, a feat he had not yet witnessed.

"Take my advice, and stay clear," was Mr Bagthorpe's parting word before going back to his study. "There's nothing that hound wouldn't stoop to."

"You've done a first-rate job on the Bear stuff," Uncle Parker told Jack as they sauntered down the garden. "Swallowed it hook, line and sinker, the lot of them. And given Grandma a new lease of life."

She had confided in him her belief that some time in the near future there was to be a Second Coming of Thomas. She had implored him to approach the house with caution in the future.

"Drive at ten miles an hour," she had pleaded, "drive at five. Give him a chance this time."

"I must say I'm not surprised they think I'm barmy," Jack told Uncle Parker. "It sounds barmy, the whole lot of it. Even to me."

"All will be revealed on the eleventh," Uncle Parker said.

"They don't really look up to me, you know, even

now," Jack continued. "They don't look at me with awe and hang on my every word, like you said they would. They take more notice of me all right, but they definitely aren't treating me like a Prophet."

"They will," he promised. "After Wednesday."

"What happened yesterday?" Jack asked him, remembering. "Was it Daisy?"

Uncle Parker nodded.

"Rooted out some matches I'd overlooked and got a blaze going in the corner of the kitchen with cereal packets. Full ones. Snap crackle and pop all over the place."

"What're you going to do?"

"I took her to see a friend of mine who's dabbled a bit in psychology," Uncle Parker said. "We're going to try Saturation."

"What's that?"

"It's letting her make fires the whole time, even making her make fires, till she's sick of the sight of them."

"Aren't you going to run out of things to set fire *to*?" asked Jack.

"Good thought. Got any old newspapers in the garage?"

Jack helped him to fetch some and stack them in the boot of his car. He could not help having his doubts about the effectiveness of this experiment. Uncle Parker had some very odd friends and their advice was not often sound. He had the kind of friends who would set off all of a sudden to travel to Katmandhu or Turkey, and then turn up months later to stay with him, bringing with them numerous half-baked theories they had picked up during their travels. Once one of them had brought Aunt Celia some worry beads, and they had disturbed her and got on her nerves so much that in the end she had deliberately snapped them, wailing, "I can't bear it, I can't!" and sent worry beads flying all over everywhere. Jack had been there at the time and knew for a fact that the only thing that had been worrying her was the worry beads. She had calmed down again the minute the worry beads had been swept up and thrown in the dustbin.

"Now don't forget," Uncle Parker told Jack before he drove off, "keep it up. Keep all three Prongs on the boil from now on. And stick to the dowsing – we're going into countdown now – five days to zero hour."

"Zero hour," repeated Jack. "Hear that, Zero?"

Zero wagged his tail in the half-hearted way he had.

"It's pretty good, having an hour named after you," Jack told him, as he watched Uncle Parker drive off in a flurry of gravel. (He was obviously not yet on the lookout for a resurrected Thomas.) "Not to mention having your portrait painted. Come on."

He went back to the house to hang around waiting

for openings for Visions, Mysterious Impressions, anything that he could pull in. He spent most of the next four days doing this. It was up to him, he knew, to create the build-up to the final revelations at Rosie's Birthday Picnic. He had the whole lot of them on the hop in the end.

He found that the minute he entered a room anyone who was in there would find some excuse to leave it almost immediately. He began to see that being a Prophet and a Phenomenon was a sad and lonely life. Even Mrs Fosdyke became uneasy when he was alone with her in the kitchen. Her nerves were already under strain with the preparations for the party fare. She took great pride in catering for special occasions and elaborately decorated everything she made. She was more than usually anxious about this particular occasion because Rosie, knowing that one of her presents was to be a camera, had told her that she intended to photograph all the food.

"If it comes out well," she told Mrs Fosdyke, "I shall get it enlarged and hang it on the wall at the side of my Birthday Self-Portrait."

The thought of having her trifle and stuffed eggs immortalised on film had Mrs Fosdyke in agonies of excitement and trepidation.

"Mind you," she told her cronies in The Fiddler's Arms (where she had taken to going most evenings of late, partly because she felt the need and partly because there had been so much news to tell), "mind you, it does give you an incentive. Every now and then I'll be in the middle of stuffing an egg or trimming up a pork pie and I'll think to myself, 'Even when it's all been eaten up, it'll still be here. It'll be here for ever –' and a fair shiver runs up me. It's having your cake and eating it, see."

There was no doubt, then, that the food for this particular birthday was going to be the best ever – certainly from the visual point of view. Mrs Fosdyke was paying great attention to doilies, and the colour of the paper napkins.

The picnic would not be a picnic in the strictest sense of the word because the meal would be laid on trestle tables and the guests would sit on chairs rather than rugs. It was Mrs Fosdyke who had pressed for this arrangement. She gave as her reason that the elder Mr and Mrs Bagthorpe would be uncomfortable seated on the ground and, if it were damp, might even damage their health. The real reason was that she wanted her culinary masterpieces photographed against the background of a lace tablecloth, not plaid travelling rugs with holes in them.

The day before the picnic Jack nearly put a fatal spanner in the works by having another Vision of the Giant Bubble and Great Brown Bear and rounding it off with the faintly uttered words:

"… tomorrow… the eleventh… tomorrow…"

Nobody much liked the sound of this. Vague and indeterminate allusions to such phenomena were one thing, but when a date was set for their appearance it threw a very different light on things.

"You realise," said Tess in a wobbly voice, "that there's a wood on the other side of that meadow, don't you? And you realise, don't you, that bears generally live in woods?"

Rosie had then squealed and said she had changed her mind and wanted the party in the dining-room even if it was all charred up. William said that if a Great Brown Bear was out to get the Bagthorpes, it would get them anyway, if he knew anything about prophecies. The whole point of a prophecy, he said, was that it was inevitable. If they went to the ends of the earth for Rosie's party, if they went to China for it, then if that Great Brown Bear was destined to get them, get them it would.

Mrs Bagthorpe told him to go up to his room after he had made this speech. She practically never sent her children to their rooms; she did not, by and large, believe in it. On the other hand she herself felt that she could not stand much more talk of this sort, and Rosie certainly could not. Jack felt really sorry for her because it was after all her birthday, and she was only going to be nine. He felt so sorry he went down into the village and bought her an extra present on top of the one he had already got for her.

Mrs Bagthorpe tried to comfort her and told her that William was only teasing. Grandma then chipped in and said she hoped not, because if anything was going to emerge from that wood tomorrow afternoon, then that thing would be Thomas, in all his old golden glory.

"I am as certain of it," she said, "as I have ever been certain of anything."

She took Jack on one side later in the day and asked him if he could possibly arrange to have another Vision and this time try to see things a little more distinctly.

"I can't just bring them on," he told her, which was true. "They just happen –" which was not. Although he enjoyed the attention he was getting Jack was beginning to get a little tired of having to evade awkward questions and even tell fibs. He was probably looking forward to the next day more than any other single member of the Bagthorpe family. If Uncle Parker's forecast was correct, his position would be once and for all established.

"And yours, Zero," he told him, as he prepared for bed that night. "Your name will live for ever."

The prospect apparently left Zero unmoved, because he flopped down by the pile of comics and put his nose between his front paws. Jack took out the Plan of Campaign and updated it. He put in details of all the Visions and Manifestations of the past few days, which took quite a long time. He ended up by writing:

Tomorrow my time will come. Even Father will lay his neck beneath my heel.

He underlined this, concealed the notebook among the comics again, and went to bed.

Chapter Fifteen

The Bagthorpes were up early on the morning of the eleventh. Rosie had made sure of this. They were all gathered in the kitchen surrounded by wrapping paper and string when Mrs Fosdyke arrived just before eight.

"Happy Birthday, Rosie." She was removing her coat as she spoke, but instead of a hat, she was wearing today a turban that almost concealed a headful of tin curlers. This she kept on. "And here's something for you."

She had given Rosie a toy xylophone that they all recognised because it had been in the village shop since the previous Christmas. (Mrs Fosdyke rarely went into the town. She said there were too many cars and that the air was pollutinated. Also, she was afraid of having her pocket picked.)

A discussion of the weather followed. It was one of those July days when the weather could swing either way. It was still cool, there was a rather watery look about the sky, but on the other hand a hint that the sun was there, about to break through. By and large, it seemed that the picnic was on. There were mixed feelings about this.

"You didn't have any dreams or anything last night, did you, Jack?" Tess asked.

He truthfully assured her that he had not, but she none the less announced her intention of taking her rounders bat down to the field with her for self-defence. She also said it was a pity that Mr Bagthorpe could not shoot.

"Most people who live in the country can shoot," she said accusingly. "You haven't even got a gun."

Mr Bagthorpe pointed out that it would be difficult to get any worthwhile kind of an aim with his right arm in plaster, and added that he didn't believe in killing animals anyway. He loved animals, he said, and was a conservationist.

Grandpa must have caught some of the drift of the conversation because he said loudly:

"Newspaper's the best. Get 'em on a clear surface and – swat!" He brought the flat of his hand down on the table to illustrate his point.

"Bit early for wasps yet," he said cheerfully, "but you never know. Make sure we take some newspapers. No harm in one of those sprays, either."

He was evidently in a happy mood at the prospect of possibly combining his two favourite pursuits (stuffed eggs were bound to be on the menu).

"I hopes, Mrs Bagthorpe," said Mrs Fosdyke, "that there will be no squirting sprays on my food."

"Of course not, Mrs Fosdyke," she assured her. "That was just Mr Bagthorpe's little joke."

It was a busy morning for everyone. William and Jack were given the job of carrying the trestle tables and chairs down to the field. Zero accompanied them on each journey and this got on William's nerves.

"That dog can't do anything," he said. "Most dogs can carry things in their mouths."

Jack pointed out that it was unreasonable to expect Zero to carry a chair in his mouth, or a trestle.

"It's not even as if he's a *guard* dog," William said. "If that Bear of yours does turn up this afternoon he'll be out of this field like a flash. He'll probably be the only one to get away."

They then had an argument about where to place the tables once they had them in the field. William wanted them in the open, Jack under a tree. William said things dropped out of trees and he didn't want things in his food, thank you, and Jack argued that if the sun came out all the cream in the meringues and strawberry shortcake and such would go sour. In the end they compromised and half was in sun, half in shade.

Mr Bagthorpe had earlier said rather smugly how he regretted not being able to help because of his injured arm, and shut himself up in his study. About mid-morning he came out again. He went into the kitchen and flung himself into a chair.

"It's happened," he announced.

"What has, dear?" Mrs Bagthorpe was packing paper cups and plates into a box.

"I've got a block," he said.

"Oh, I'm sure you haven't, dear," said Mrs Bagthorpe. She went on counting under her breath and this must have irritated Mr Bagthorpe, who liked to have a serious thing like a block *taken* seriously.

"It's the end of the road," he said tragically. "I've lost it. It's gone."

"Lost what?" enquired Mrs Bagthorpe absentmindedly. "Eleven, twelve, thirteen—"

"Lost whatever it was I had, of course!" Mr Bagthorpe was beginning to shout. "You don't understand. None of you understand."

As if to rub salt in the wound Mrs Fosdyke was bustling about the place, darting from here to there in her best hedgehog manner. Every available surface was taken up with trays of food. Mr Bagthorpe glowered at her. It seemed to him a bitter irony that he was blocked and Mrs Fosdyke was not. Mrs Fosdyke, indeed, was on peak form.

Matters were not improved by Grandma entering at this juncture, carrying a dusty-looking cat basket.

"Tess found it in the loft and is going to clean it up for me and line it with flannel," she told them. "Everything will be ready."

Mr Bagthorpe opened his mouth to make a cutting retort, then remembered it was someone's birthday, and closed it again. He really did make an effort to be calm and kind on feast days. He did not think he could manage it surrounded by people darting about like hedgehogs, however, or crooning over tattered cat baskets, so he left abruptly to hug his block to himself. He went into the sitting-room and found Rosie there, seated before a mirror, painting her Birthday Self-Portrait.

"Oh, do go away," she begged. "I can't do it if anyone's looking."

He could not bear the sterile atmosphere of his study, jibbed at the charred dining-room, so went into the garden, where he began dead-heading roses to calm his nerves.

The party was due to begin at half past three with family games in the meadow, followed by tea. Lunch was an almost non-existent affair, with people walking about with cheese sandwiches and talking with their mouths full. No one could sit at a table because the tables were all covered with trays of food for tea.

At two Mrs Fosdyke excused herself and went up to the bathroom carrying a large black plastic bag. When she came down ten minutes later she was transformed. Her hair was in tight curls, she wore a black dress with sprays of mauve flowers on it and shiny shoes with heels. The Bagthorpes boggled. They had never seen Mrs Fosdyke dressed up before. Even at parties – perhaps *especially* at parties – she would always run around in her wrap-round pinafore, giving an impression of ten people doing the work of one. On these previous occasions, of course, Mrs Fosdyke had never had the prospect of being photographed with her food. As Mr Bagthorpe afterwards remarked, you never saw Fanny Craddock in a wrap-round pinafore with her hair in curlers.

None of the Bagthorpes had intended to do anything very special in the way of dress. The kind of games they were proposing to play were of the rough and tumble variety, and although no one put this into words, no one wished to be caught fleeing from a Great Brown Bear in long skirts, or any other form of clothing that might impede rapid movement. Now, however, they felt that Mrs Fosdyke had set a certain tone, which it was up to them to match.

One by one, therefore, they drifted upstairs and came down attired with a greater or lesser degree of sartorial elegance. Grandma put on an old black full-length frock and a silver locket which everybody knew contained two colour photographs of Thomas. Not to be outdone, all the other female Bagthorpes wore long skirts, with the sole exception of Tess, who was obviously more worried about the Great Brown Bear than anyone else. She wore a pair of new denim flares she had been saving for going on holiday. William, doubtless with the intention of impressing Atlanta, and giving himself a Byronic air, wore a purple shirt with a yellow scarf knotted carelessly at the neck – a style he had never previously gone in for. Oddly enough, Mr Bagthorpe had opted for much the same sort of thing, and the pair of them kept eyeing one another hard, as if each was suspecting the other of some kind of subversive tactic.

When Uncle Parker roared up at about three, himself attired in a cream open-necked shirt with a scarlet neckerchief, the whole thing really did begin to look like a conspiracy or the beginnings of a secret society. Jack was reminded of what Mrs Fosdyke had said about things always going in threes. He took a good look at Daisy and thought she looked rather calm and subdued. Perhaps the Saturation technique had taken all the fire-raising spirit out of her. He hoped so. He did not know what it was that was to happen shortly in the meadow, but whatever it was he did not want it distracted from by something going up in flames. Aunt Celia was wearing sunglasses although the sun was not fully out. Jack thought perhaps she felt safer behind them. If she'd known about the Great Brown Bear it was unlikely that she would have been present at all, he thought. She must simply be suffering from an understandable general sense of unease.

Once they were all foregathered Mrs Bagthorpe arranged a kind of ceremonial procession down to the meadow with everyone carrying a tray of food, and Rosie in the lead bearing the cake. Mrs Fosdyke insisted on carrying the trifles and the strawberry shortcake herself. Obviously she felt these were the most photogenic of her efforts and did not wish to see them end up in the long grass. Grandpa had been entrusted with the stuffed eggs and was walking very carefully indeed, his eyes fixed on them.

The food was laid out, with Mrs Fosdyke darting hither and thither putting little finishing touches, and then the Bagthorpes stood back to watch the photograph being taken. The sun came out, right on cue.

"I should take more than one, dear," Mrs Fosdyke said, nervously patting her curls, "just in case it don't come out. You never know with cameras."

"I'll take three," Rosie told her. "One at each end of the table and one in the middle, and then we'll get everything in."

Mrs Fosdyke was so enchanted by this news that when she posed she actually did look happy – something she hardly ever allowed herself to do. For one of the photographs she picked up a plate of her meringues and held it, looking for all the world like a proud mother at a christening. After the photographs all the Bagthorpes clapped, and Mrs Fosdyke must have been really touched because she actually dabbed at her eyes with a paper napkin. Only Mr Bagthorpe seemed discontented. Mrs Fosdyke was having a gala performance, and he was blocked.

Two large white cloths were then spread over the food to protect it while the games were going on. They did not get off to a very good start because so many people were opting out. Grandma elected to sit on a chair facing the wood, keeping a sharp lookout for the imminent second coming of Thomas. Mr Bagthorpe said that his head and his arm were aching, and flung himself full length on the ground in a Greek pose, looking mean and moody. Grandpa made a game attempt but obviously could not hear half the instructions that were bawled at him. A portable wireless had been brought out for musical chairs, and Grandpa just seemed to be sitting when the fancy took him, regardless of whether or not the music had stopped.

None the less those who were participating in the games became increasingly excited and giggly and no one took any notice of Mr Bagthorpe, who kept looking at his watch, and then at the covered table.

"Would it be *very* antisocial," he said at last, "as I am precluded by my injury from taking part in the merriment, if I went and fetched a book? It is not in my nature to sit idling around, and I could be doing some serious reading."

No one objected, and off he went. The games continued, reaching a climax with Blind Man's Buff, in which William put his foot down a rabbit hole and was so put out at looking silly in front of Atlanta that his unfeeling relatives were reduced to near-hysteria. Mrs Fosdyke had joined in one or two of the quieter games, but now kept taking quick peeks under the cloth to see how her food was bearing up.

"I do think, Mrs Bagthorpe," she said eventually, "that tea should be served, if we don't wish icing melted, and such."

"Of course!" Mrs Bagthorpe clapped her hands. Everyone ran to the table and sat down and the covers were taken off.

The meal was a triumph. In no way had aesthetic considerations been allowed to interfere with the gastronomic aspect of the food, as had been feared in some quarters. Mrs Fosdyke was showered with crumb-choked compliments. She herself sat down with them at Rosie's right hand; and really seemed, just for the moment, a member of the family.

Everyone, even Grandma and Tess, seemed to have forgotten entirely the Giant Bubble and the Great Brown Bear. Uncle Parker seemed relaxed and flippant and did not catch Jack's eye once, even though he was sitting diagonally opposite.

He can't have forgotten, Jack thought. *It was his idea in the first place.*

If he *had* forgotten, it seemed to Jack that he might have to leave home, taking Zero with him. The time for pulling the crackers came and still nothing had manifested.

"There's a couple spare!" exclaimed Uncle Parker, holding them up. (They all had two crackers each, to make up for the disaster at Grandma's party – and to provide, of course, double the number of mottoes.)

"Henry!" cried Mrs Bagthorpe. "He hasn't come back!"

None of the Bagthorpes had noticed his absence up to this point – surprisingly, really, because his presence was of the kind that was usually felt – and correspondingly missed.

"He went to fetch a book," she said. "I expect he became engrossed in it. Poor Henry."

"We may as well pull his crackers for him," suggested Uncle Parker. "He may not want to pull them left-handed."

"No," said Rosie with unexpected firmness. "Leave them alone. They're his."

Uncle Parker obediently replaced them by the empty plate. There were shrieks and bangs for quite a long time then, and right in the middle of it all Jack felt a sharp kick on his ankle.

"Ouch!" he exclaimed. "What—?"

Uncle Parker opposite frowned warningly, then jerked his head. Jack followed the direction of his gaze.

"Crikey!" he said, though nobody heard him, being so involved with crackers and all reading mottoes at the tops of their voices.

Floating gracefully just above the tips of the trees was a huge red and white striped air balloon. It came serenely and silently in the blue, in a world apart, it seemed, from the noisy, earthbound Bagthorpes. Jack gaped. He could see the flames of the gas, and, above the edge of the basket, not one, but two Great Brown Bears. Still he stared.

There was a piercing scream.

"Look!" screeched Tess. "Look at Jack! He's seeing something!"

"Nonsense, darling," Mrs Bagthorpe started to say and then her voice trailed off. She too was staring, and all the party turned their heads in the direction of her gaze, with the exception of Grandpa who was blissfully putting away what it seemed could very well be his last ever stuffed egg.

In the hush that followed all that could be heard was the hissing of the gas as the Giant Bubble approached.

Uncle Parker rose to his feet.

"Jack," he said solemnly, "I take my hat off to you."

"Oh, Mummy," whimpered Rosie, and ran from her chair. "Look – there's two enormous bears!"

"Now, darling." Mrs Bagthorpe's voice trembled ever so slightly. "Keep calm. I think they may be friendly. Look – yes, they're waving."

"They're definitely not Thomas!" Grandma sounded sad and suddenly old. She was not scared, just really disappointed. "Oh, Thomas!"

The bears were not only waving but scattering what looked like visiting cards over the far side of the meadow as they left the wood behind. The Bagthorpes sat mesmerised. Slowly the balloon drifted towards them. It seemed to be losing height.

"If they land," quavered Tess, "I shall just shut my eyes and hope to die. I can't bear it."

"So dangerous… not really…" murmured Aunt Celia

who, oddly, seemed not nearly so distraught as might have been expected. Only Jack noted this, however. The others were all too busy being distraught themselves.

Atlanta was jabbering away excitedly in Danish and pointing to the balloon and then at herself. She seemed to be trying to tell them that it was herself it was coming for.

"Look," said William to Jack, "can you tell them to go away?"

Jack stood up.

"I might," he said, not really knowing.

"You can speak to Anonymous from Grimsby any time you want to."

"Thanks." Jack was not really listening. He now had the impression that something was wrong in the Giant Bubble. The Great Brown Bears had stopped dropping visiting cards and were scuffling about inside the basket and shouting in what sounded suspiciously like human voices. The balloon *was* losing height. It looked rather as though it was going to land right in the middle of the table.

"If they land," William said, "I shall go up this tree and take Atlanta with me."

"B-b-bears c-can climb trees," Tess quavered.

"I'm glad those photos got took, anyway," came Mrs Fosdyke's small voice.

The basket was rocking now and bags were being thrown out of it. The hissing of the gas seemed fainter, though the balloon was up close now, a bare hundred yards away.

At this point Uncle Parker cupped his hands and bawled: "Keep up! Keep up! What's the matter with you?"

Another couple of bags fell with a thud. The Great Brown Bears were so close now that you could see the whites of their eyes, almost. They looked very worried bears, so far as Jack could judge.

"For crying out loud!" bawled Uncle Parker. "What's the game?"

There was a final, sighing hiss, a gentle folding and settling of the Giant Bubble, and the whole thing came down. The basket rocked wildly and the Bagthorpes rose as one and prepared to run. Uncle Parker was the only one present who kept his cool. He advanced towards the basket, where the two Great Brown Bears were scrambling out and now stood upright, brushing down their fur.

"Hail, O Great Brown Bears," he greeted them.

"Oh! Isn't he brave!" gasped Mrs Bagthorpe.

Uncle Parker gave a kind of half-bow in salute and the Great Brown Bears did likewise in a clumsy kind of way.

"I think they might be tame," whispered Tess.

"You have come with a Message?" Uncle Parker asked

the question in a loud, ceremonial voice such as is used at coronations and the opening of Parliament.

The two Great Brown Bears nodded portentously.

"You have come, perhaps, to tell us who is the Chosen One?"

Again they nodded.

Uncle Parker turned.

"Quick – Jack – here!"

Jack advanced doubtfully.

"Can you identify who is Chosen?" asked Uncle Parker.

The larger of the two Great Brown Bears lifted a huge furry paw and pointed. The other, after a moment's hesitation, followed suit. They were pointing, unmistakably, to Jack.

To say that the Bagthorpes were struck all of a heap would not be to do justice to their state. They were used to excitement in large doses. They were about as hardened as any family in England could be to chaos and catastrophe and even the downright impossible. But this was too much. It seemed as if they might have remained rooted for ever when a shout came from behind them.

"Here! Here! What—?"

Wisely, none of the Bagthorpes removed their eyes from the Great Brown Bears. They recognised the voice well enough.

"Get them!" yelled Mr Bagthorpe. "Grab hold of those bears before they make off!"

The Bagthorpes ignored this mystifying instruction. Everybody, including the Bears, seemed fixed now in a kind of tableau. The only movement was the gentle billowing of the red and white balloon. The only sound was the thudding of Mr Bagthorpe's feet on the turf. He thundered, astonishingly, right past the lot of them, past Uncle Parker and Jack, and came to a halt nose to nose, almost, with the Great Brown Bears, who actually backed away from him.

"Oh, Father!" breathed Tess ecstatically.

"Henry!" Mrs Bagthorpe stepped forward with a faint cry.

"You get those damn-fool heads off!" Mr Bagthorpe was yelling. "You hear me? Get those heads off. Let's see who you are!"

Some kind of game was apparently up. The Bears seemed to be looking enquiringly at Uncle Parker, who was slowly nodding his head. In unison four clumsy paws went up and two great furry heads were lifted clean off. A bald-headed man and one with a beard stood awkwardly holding their erstwhile heads under their arms.

"Sorry, Russell, old chap," said the one with the beard. "Gas ran out. No wind. One of those things."

At this point Atlanta rushed forward and amazingly embraced the bearded man and began babbling excitedly in Danish.

"Oooh," said Mrs Fosdyke. "I think I'm going to faint."

She refrained from doing so probably only out of curiosity. The account she would give later in the Fiddler's Arms ought not to have any gaps in it.

Mr Bagthorpe turned now to face Uncle Parker and Jack. He had something in his hand.

"What about this then?" he shouted. "What about all *this*?"

He flung whatever it was he was holding at Jack. It fell right at his feet. It was a small red loose-leafed notebook. It was the Plan of Campaign. Jack dared not raise his eyes.

"Whose neck under *whose* heel?" yelled Mr Bagthorpe.

Then, miraculously, one of the two visitors let out a yell.

"Fire! Hey, look – fire!"

The Bagthorpes whirled about. From the direction of the summer house thick blue smoke was issuing above the trees. All hell was instantly let loose. Everyone present, even Aunt Celia, started at top speed in the direction of the smoke. Mrs Fosdyke brought up the rear, saying over and over again:

"Threes – things always go in threes. Threes – things always go in threes."

(She did not, of course, know that Daisy had lit a good many more fires than three – she was by now well into double figures and getting better all the time.)

Jack, alone, picked up the little book and set off slowly after them. Daisy, again, had saved the day. But for how long?

Epilogue

When the final reckoning came to be made, Jack did not emerge so badly as he had feared. It turned out that his greatest inspiration had been to conceal the Plan of Campaign in the pile of despised comics. Indeed, had Mr Bagthorpe been a less impulsive man, he would have taken thought before rushing down to the meadow brandishing the incriminating evidence he had found. He had, after all, found it only because he had been steadily wading his way through the back numbers of Jack's comics.

Having the entire Bagthorpe household aware of this took the wind to a very great extent out of his sails. He was never, indeed, quite allowed to forget it. In unmasking Uncle Parker's and Jack's plot, he had at the same time made an eternal rod for his own back. He quietened down a lot. He shouted less. The rest of the Bagthorpes did not fail to notice this softening of his character, and were accordingly grateful to Jack.

It had, when all was said and done, been only boyish mischief. This was what Mrs Bagthorpe said when she had bewilderedly collected the whole story. She even said how imaginative and bold it had all been. She did not say this till several days later, but after that she said it quite a lot, and even told Jack that she was, in a way, proud of him.

Grandma, though disappointed at the non-reappearance of Thomas, had on the whole enjoyed the whole charade. She said that at her age you didn't get frightened of things any more. You have seen everything, she said, and what had taken place in the meadow had been, so far as she was concerned, simply another warp in the web of life's rich pattern. She stated that she was speaking for Grandpa as well when she said this, and as he himself never alluded to it, perhaps she was.

Rosie, in retrospect, became overweeningly proud that her Birthday Party had been the greatest and best Bagthorpian party of all times, leaving even Grandma's débâcle nowhere. She had used the rest of her film taking photographs of the Giant Bubble and the Great Brown

Bears, both with and without their heads. She had also collected a lot, though not all, of the visiting cards they had dropped, which turned out to be pieces of white card with the words JACK BAGTHORPE APPOINTED PROPHET printed on them. These she had had signed by the two Great Brown Bears and then pasted into her autograph album. All in all, she had had a very gratifying day as far as keeping records was concerned.

Mrs Fosdyke had at first marched off to write a letter giving in her notice. But when she came out to give it to Mrs Bagthorpe, she had found the fire put out and the whole party reassembled round the table, having not yet lit the candles and sung 'Happy Birthday' to Rosie – an obvious piece of unfinished business. The two bears had then paid her such fulsome compliments about her food, and tucked into it with such gratifying enthusiasm, that she stuffed the letter back in her pocket and decided on this occasion to give the Bagthorpes the credit of some very dubious goings-on. She later said in The Fiddler's Arms that she thought the two bears had been "proper gentlemen" and gave it out that the real culprit was Uncle Parker, who was also, she said, cold-blooded and with a very queer sense of humour indeed.

"Nobody," she opined, "after goings-on like that – and a fire to crown all – would've else been crawling about like a two-year-old on his hands and knees picking up mottoes out of crackers, I ask you!"

Mottoes out of crackers, she went on to say, were not even funny, whereas Uncle Parker decidedly was – in the head.

Uncle Parker himself, of course, was quite able to cope with this kind of adverse opinion, and was on balance highly satisfied with the way the whole thing had passed off. He was also able to explain a few otherwise incomprehensible things, like why the men in the balloon had to be disguised as bears. It was, of course, because of that Danish girl. She had been staying with old Brent, *and* knew that he had a balloon, and he couldn't risk her spilling it out and ruining the whole thing.

"She did, actually," Jack told him. "I remember now. But luckily, she did it in Danish."

"Only one cracker motto missing," Uncle Parker told him cheerfully, "and given the whole lot of 'em something to think about."

"It's all over with the Prophet and Phenomenon though, isn't it?" said Jack.

"It is, yes. But there you are – all for the best. You wouldn't have wanted to keep all that stuff up for ever, would you?"

Jack agreed that he would not.

"I prefer being ordinary Jack," he said. "Except that I don't think I'm quite as ordinary as I was before, do you? Thank you, Uncle Parker."

"Don't mention it," Uncle Parker replied gracefully. "It was a pleasure. Your father – locked away up there all afternoon reading back numbers of comics! It's you, old chap, who have done *me* a favour. I have a trump card that will never fail. The last word to end all last words."

And so gradually life in the Bagthorpe household returned to normal, or as near normal as it was ever likely to be, and Jack and Zero (who could at least now fetch sticks) lived happily for several weeks after. They lived, that is, *more* happily, because Prophet and Phenomenon or not, Jack was not, for the time being, thought of as ordinary. He was an equal. And that made Zero equal too.

COLLINS MODERN *CLASSICS*

COLLINS MODERN *CLASSICS*

COLLINS MODERN *CLASSICS*

COLLINS MODERN *CLASSICS*

COLLINS MODERN *CLASSICS*